"Who kissed who first?" Maya demanded.

"What difference does it make, since it won't ever happen again?" Adam responded angrily.

"No? What do you think about this?" She grabbed his head and yanked him down to plant a kiss on his lips, then pushed him away. "Don't you tell *me* who I will or won't kiss!"

"Don't push your luck with me, Maya!"

"No? What will you do?"

He jerked her to him and kissed her hard.

"How dare you!" she sputtered in rage. "Of all the gall!" She backed away from him, her fists clenched.

"I wouldn't keep backing up if I were you," he warned.

"No? This is *my* world, Adam Russell—or whoever you are! I do as I please!"

"Suit yourself." He folded his arms over his chest and gave her a maddening smile.

Just to prove her point, Maya took another step back. The heel of her boot found only air, and for a moment she teetered on the bank, then tumbled into the shallow river. She came up soaked and furious.

"I told you not to back up," he said mildly.

Dear Reader,

Sophisticated but sensitive, savvy yet unabashedly sentimental—that's today's woman, today's romance reader—you! And Silhouette Special Editions are written expressly to reward your quest for substantial, emotionally involving love stories.

So take a leisurely stroll under the cover's lavender arch into a garden of romantic delights. Pick and choose among titles if you must—we hope you'll soon equate all six Special Editions each month with consistently gratifying romantic reading.

Watch for sparkling new stories from your Silhouette favorites—Nora Roberts, Tracy Sinclair, Ginna Gray, Lindsay McKenna, Curtiss Ann Matlock, among others—along with some exciting newcomers to Silhouette, such as Karen Keast and Patricia Coughlin. Be on the lookout, too, for the new Silhouette Classics, a distinctive collection of bestselling Special Editions and Silhouette Intimate Moments now brought back to the stands—two each month—by popular demand.

On behalf of all the authors and editors of Special Editions,
Warmest wishes,

Leslie Kazanjian
Senior Editor

LYNDA TRENT
Heat Lightning

Silhouette Special Edition

Published by Silhouette Books New York

America's Publisher of Contemporary Romance

SILHOUETTE BOOKS
300 East 42nd St., New York, N.Y. 10017

Copyright © 1988 by Dan and Lynda Trent

All rights reserved, including the right to reproduce
this book or portions thereof in any form whatsoever.
For information address Silhouette Books,
300 East 42nd St., New York, N.Y. 10017

ISBN: 0-373-09443-4

First Silhouette Books printing March 1988

America's Publisher of Contemporary Romance

Printed in the U.S.A.

LYNDA TRENT

started writing romances at the insistence of a friend, but it was her husband who provided moral support whenever her resolve flagged. Now husband and wife are both full-time writers of contemporary and historical novels, and despite the ups and downs of this demanding career, they love every—well, *almost* every—minute of it.

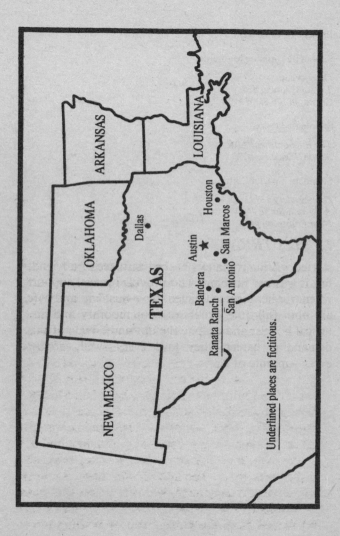

ARKANSAS

LOUISIANA

OKLAHOMA

Houston

Dallas

San Marcos

Austin ★

San Antonio

TEXAS

Bandera

San Antonio

Ranata Ranch

NEW MEXICO

Underlined places are fictitious.

Prologue

The high-pitched whine of a motorcycle sliced
through the hot silence of the Texas hill country as its
lone rider squinted under the sweltering July sun.
Ahead of him the heat danced over the ribbon of road,
creating watery mirages in its hollows. He consulted
his wristwatch again and peered across the landscape
studded with cactus and juniper. There was no sign of
civilization, and by his reckoning he already should
have crossed Interstate 10 on his way to San Marcos.

Philip looked down at the gauges on the cycle and
frowned. The motor was running hot, and he was low
on fuel. He should have refueled in Bandera and not
tried to make it all the way to San Marcos, especially
on this back route. Too late for that now. Again he
looked past the sagging barbed-wire fences that lined
the road to arid pastureland strewn with yellow rocks
and shaded from the blazing sun by nothing larger

than mesquite trees. This didn't look like the San
Marcos area at all.

The farther he rode, the narrower the road became,
until it was little more than a single lane of blacktop.
He eased off on the throttle and drifted to a stop under a mesquite tree. This was definitely the wrong way.
He stood and pulled a neatly folded map from the
back pocket of his jeans and spread it out on the han-
dlebars to study it. There was Kerrville, and south-
east of it was the road he'd planned to take. So where
was San Marcos?

A fat fly hummed lazily as it circled Philip's head,
and he brushed at it impatiently. He wasn't worried;
in this part of Texas a person could top a rise and discover a fertile valley, even a town, without knowing
one was anywhere around. Philip was more upset that
his carefully planned schedule was already off kilter.
Although he had plenty of vacation time, there was a
lot he wanted to accomplish. As he refolded the map
he had to admit that Sally had been right; he should
have taken his car. It might not have kept him from
taking that shortcut out of Bandera, but he would
have been cooler while trying to find his way back.

He revved the motorcycle and turned back the way
he had come. There was a fork in the road not too far
back. He would try the other route.

In an hour the sun was almost directly overhead,
beating pitilessly on his helmet. Rivulets of sweat
streamed down his face. The wind whipping his blue
cambric shirt kept him from overheating, but he
wondered at times if his judgment might be impaired.
Instead of taking that fork in the road, he should have
headed back exactly as he had come and returned to
Kerrville.

The motorcycle coughed and missed a beat. Philip looked down in consternation. It had been running hot for miles, and now the fuel-gauge needle was dead on empty. The engine missed again and began to slow.

Philip called the machine a few choice names as it coasted to a stop beside an outcropping of cactus-shrouded rock. A gnarled cedar tree, alive only at the tip, curved up from a crevice in the rock like a huge snake that had been trapped in the stone. He turned off the key and sat there for a minute, wondering what to do next. The heat and the silence were overwhelming. Even the birds seemed to have taken shelter.

Taking a conservative sip from his canteen, Philip looked around. He couldn't see far in any direction because of the rolling hills. The dust settled around him, leaving a film of dull yellow on his clothing and boots. There were no cows in sight, no line of river willows to indicate a stream, certainly no hint of civilization except for the narrow black road and the sagging barbed-wire fences.

Conditioned to city life, Philip pushed his expensive motorcycle behind a clump of mesquite so it wouldn't be stolen before he could return for it. Taking careful note of the peculiarly-shaped cedar in the rock as the most distinctive landmark around, he started walking.

Knowing there was nothing for miles behind him, he headed in the direction he had been driving. In this case, he thought, the unknown was better than the known.

The road was hot under the soles of his boots, so he walked in the dirt beside the pavement. Occasionally he heard a slithering sound as a lizard ran for cover— he refused to think it might be a snake. He had left his helmet on his motorcycle, which he soon realized was a mistake. The sun bore down on his bare head with a ferocity that made his eyes sting.

A couple of times he was positive he saw water ahead—only to realize it was another mirage. He licked his dry lips and narrowed his eyes. Still no one in sight. He trudged on.

Although he was sparing with his water, the canteen was empty by late afternoon. The sun had dropped halfway to the trees and now shone in his eyes rather than just on the top of his head. That meant he was going west instead of east as he had intended. The winding road must have doubled back on him while the sun was high in the sky and he hadn't been able to distinguish the change in direction. Philip knew by the stinging of his skin that he must be badly burned, but there was nothing he could do. He didn't dare stop walking to seek out shade because he had no idea how far he had yet to go.

By dusk his steps were faltering, and he knew he was in trouble. The slightly cooler air did little to revive him. The backs of his hands were fiery red, and his face felt at least that burned. His ears were humming, and it took several seconds before he realized the noise wasn't in his head.

He looked back to see an old car coming toward him. His lips moved, but no sound came from his parched throat. With a supreme effort he forced himself to shout and wave his arms.

The car swerved as if to go around him, and for a moment he thought it would pass him by. Then the vehicle slowed and stopped. Philip pushed himself to a stumbling trot and grabbed the door handle, as if that would prevent the driver from leaving him behind.

"Hey, man. What's going on?" a Mexican man asked as he peered up at Philip.

"I ran out of gas. Can you give me a ride to town?" He leaned heavily on the car and hoped he didn't look as disreputable as he felt.

The Mexican turned to the driver and said with a laugh, "He says he wants a ride. What do you think about that?"

The driver, a white youth with a straggly mustache, leaned over to look at Philip's face. "I ain't seen no car back there, man. What town you headed to?"

"Anywhere. It doesn't matter."

The passenger winked at his buddy. "I reckon we can give him a ride. Don't you?"

"Sure!" the other drawled in exaggerated enthusiasm. "Let him in."

The Mexican got out and motioned for Philip to sit between them. A warning bell rang in Philip's head, but he ignored it. There might not be another car along this road for days. He slid in and nearly gagged on the smell of beer, tobacco and unwashed bodies. Still, it was a ride. "How far is it to town?" he asked as the car lurched forward.

"Well, now, that depends on which town," the Mexican said. "Nuevo Laredo, she's a long way off. Los Angeles, she's even farther."

"How far to San Marcos?"

The men laughed as if he had made a joke. "You can't get there from here, man."

Philip's uneasiness was becoming tinged with worry. "You don't have anything to drink, do you? A jug of water, maybe?"

"Water! Hell, I ain't touched water in years! That'll rust your gut, man."

"We had some beer, but it's gone now," the driver said.

Philip tried to relax. Probably these were two rough cowhands out to celebrate a Saturday paycheck and nothing more threatening than that.

The Mexican leaned forward and pointed to a side road. "Turn here."

"Here?" the driver repeated.

"Just do what I tell you."

Philip's concern sharpened into cold apprehension. "Is town this way?" When they both laughed, he began to wonder if he could talk his way out of this. "Look, you've helped me enough. Just let me out here, and I'll find my own way."

"We can't do that, man. We couldn't forgive ourselves." He leaned across Philip to poke the driver. "Ain't that right?"

"That's right, man."

They topped a rise, and the road dipped sharply into shadow. The sun had already set, and night was settling into the low spots. The car rolled to a stop, and Philip looked around. There wasn't a light in sight. "Where are we?"

"We got something to show you, man. Won't take but a minute." The Mexican got out and held the door for Philip as the driver slid out the other side.

Normally Philip was in excellent condition and quite capable of defending himself. Now, however, he was exhausted, suffering from the heat and dehydration, and there were two of them. When the Mexican swung at him, Philip stepped aside and grabbed at the man's hand but missed. He braced himself, but they circled him, and the driver managed to pin his arms behind him.

Philip struggled as the Mexican closed in but could do nothing to stop the fist that slammed into his face.

When Philip came to, he was lying facedown in the middle of a dirt road, and all around was darkness. The only sounds he heard were those of insects singing. He tried to get up but the pain made him drop back down to the road.

After a bit he tried again, and this time he was able to stumble to his feet. He squinted against nauseating pain as he weaved unsteadily. He had to find help.

Doggedly he started walking, forcing one foot in front of the other, using all his willpower to keep moving.

After what seemed an eternity, he saw a light. He swayed as he changed his course to head directly for it. Not daring to look away lest his only hope vanish, he pushed himself forward.

Chapter One

Maya Kingsley sipped cool Chablis from a hand-blown glass and leaned back on the white leather sofa. From far off in the kitchen she could hear Lupe singing a Spanish song as she finished her daily chores. Maya liked this time of evening. Sunset brought a release from the sweltering heat, and her daily responsibilities were fulfilled. It was a time of suspension between the activity that consumed her day and the emptiness of the night.

She loved the Ranata, the sprawling *rancho* that had been in her family for generations. Part of the *hacienda* was the original adobe structure her great-great-grandfather had built when he was carving out his empire. Before her parents' deaths, they had added to the house, harmonizing the new lines with the old so that the twentieth-century additions preserved the antique charm of the ancestral home. The newer walls had been built as thick as the original ones to maintain the rooms at a bearable temperature both winter and summer.

The Ranata spread over several thousand acres and required a considerable staff to keep it running smoothly. The *rancho* was almost self-sustaining, with a resident doctor and a general store, both of them necessary since the nearest town was nearly an hour away.

Managing a spread such as this was a full-time job, which kept Maya's days occupied. But nighttime was another matter; then the household servants and other employees retired to their adobe homes beyond the main house. Maya was never afraid—she knew all her people, and not one of them would harm her. On the outside chance of some stranger breaking in, there were alarms in every room that would summon her foreman and the others. Maya's only enemy was loneliness.

As a girl she had come to love the magnificence of the wide-open spaces and the special beauty that could be found in a twist of the river that meandered through the Ranata or in the blooms of the wild cacti. She had detested every minute she had had to spend at school, and as soon as she'd been awarded her college degree she had headed straight back to the Ranata. While her parents were alive, the parties had been numerous and the house often filled with guests from all over the world. But now they were gone, and the big house was still.

Restlessly Maya crossed the room and opened the sliding-glass door to her semienclosed patio. Finding the night as cool outside as it was in, she stepped out and left the door open behind her. The covered portion of the patio served as an outdoor living room, and beyond the roofline was a lagoon-shaped pool with a recirculating waterfall that spilled musically over native rocks. A gentle breeze created by the natural convection of air through the house lifted the hem of her loose white silk tunic top and pressed the wide trousers to her legs. Maya decided that as soon as Lupe left for the evening, she would go for a swim. No one would be there to see her if she went without her swimsuit, and maybe the exercise would tire her so that she could sleep.

Hearing a noise, she called over her shoulder, "Lupe?"

When she got no answer, she assumed it to be her imagination and turned her attention back to the pool. The unusual shape had been her idea, and she was glad she had talked her parents into it. A more stylized one would have fit into the setting better, perhaps, but Maya loved having the lushness of her own private lagoon. A Pisces, she was drawn to water with an obsession that would seem to belie her love for the arid Texas hill country.

Maya tilted her head back to allow the slight breeze to ripple through the heavy black curtain of her long hair. Through the thin soles of her leather sandals she felt the coolness of the handmade tiles. She couldn't imagine ever wanting to live anywhere else.

Again she heard a noise. "Lupe? Is that you?" Curious, she stepped back inside and listened. Once more she heard it. Was it a knock? Heading for the front door, she went down the hall that bordered one side of the patio. The hallway afforded no view of the front of the house, since it faced west, and there were no windows on that outside wall.

When the faint knock sounded again, she turned the ornate handle and swung open the heavy door. A man stood silhouetted in the porch light. Blood matted his blond hair, and dirt was smeared over his torn clothing. He seemed about to speak, but all at once his knees buckled and he fell through the doorway.

Maya immediately slapped the button next to the door that would signal for help, then knelt beside the man. "Are you all right?" she asked inanely as he pushed himself to a sitting position. She saw her maid hurrying in and said, "Lupe, get some water."

By the time her foreman, Javier García, arrived, Maya was steadying the glass of water for the stranger. "Get the doctor," she ordered.

"Are you sure . . . ?"

"He's in no condition to harm me. Hurry!"

In Spanish, Lupe said to her husband, "Go on, Javier. I'll watch over the *patrona*."

The man on the floor looked up at her, and Maya found herself gazing into the greenest eyes she had ever seen. Although a bruise was purpling the skin over one eyebrow, she was struck by the gentleness in his eyes. Instinctively she trusted him, and he seemed to feel the same for her, because he let her guide the glass to his bruised lips again.

Javier came running back with the doctor, and both squatted on the tile floor beside the man. The doctor, a middle-aged man who had retired to the Ranata, took the stranger's pulse. "I can't examine him here."

"Take him to the guest room," Maya said quickly. "Lupe, run and get the bed ready."

Javier slipped his sinewy arms under the man and hoisted him to his feet. Leaning heavily on the Mexican, the stranger managed to stumble down the hall

and through the library to the back room. Javier eased
him onto the edge of the bed as Lupe flipped the covers back.

"Can you sit up?" the doctor asked.

"Yes," the man answered, looking around as if he
had lost something but couldn't tell for sure just what.

"I'm a doctor," the older man was saying. "Dr.
Garth Kadlecek. Have you been in an accident?"

"I...I don't know." The man touched his head and
looked at his bloody fingers in surprise. Why was he
sitting in this room with all these people staring at him
with such concern? He tried to move, but the pain that
shot through his head stilled him.

"Here," the young woman said. She knelt beside
him and wiped his face with a cool, damp cloth. He
tried not to flinch when she touched the cut.

The doctor leaned nearer. "I don't think you need
more than a couple of stitches here. What's your
name?"

The man's eyes widened, and he opened his mouth
to answer, but he found he had no idea of his name.
With growing alarm, he tried to recall anything. Anything at all. For all he could remember, he had no history beyond this room. He couldn't even recall how he
got here. Panic began to well up in him, and only with
great difficulty did he manage to control it. His name.
He must have a name! He felt in his pockets, but they
were empty.

"What's wrong?" the doctor asked suspiciously.

"Nothing!" Everyone had a name and memories!
He felt vaguely nauseated by his confusing thoughts.

"Take off your shirt and shoes and lie down. Let's
see if you're hurt anywhere else."

He stood and shakily removed his shirt. Surreptitiously he glanced at the label, but it told him nothing except that he was a size large.

"You've got some bruises here on your abdomen." The doctor probed his muscle-ridged belly. "That hurt?"

The man flinched. "A little."

"It should. Looks like somebody worked you over good. Course it could have been a wreck. Were you in an accident?"

Had he been? He couldn't remember. He only knew it was important to give answers, to pretend he was as normal as they were—to hide the fact that he had no name. Again he reached for his empty pockets.

He felt the doctor run his fingers down the sole of his foot, and his large toe flexed. "No Babinski's reflex."

"Is that bad?"

"Nope. That's good."

The doctor opened his black bag. "Let's put a couple of stitches in this forehead."

Across the room the man saw the Mexican couple and the woman in white. She was incredibly beautiful, almost like a movie star. He must know her—why else was he sitting in her bedroom? He tried to smile at her reassuringly. She could tell him who he was once the others were gone.

As the doctor worked, he said, "Do you know what year this is?"

"Of course. It's 1988."

"What month is it?"

"May."

"Nope. It's July."

"I meant to say July."

"What day of the week is it?"

"Tuesday."

"It's Saturday. Do you remember my name?"

"Yes," he snapped. "You're Dr. Garth Kadlecek, and it's Saturday, July of '88."

"Good, good. My name's not easy to recall under the best of circumstances. What's your name?"

He glanced at the beautiful woman, but she was obviously waiting to hear it herself. He touched his belt buckle as he searched the emptiness of his mind. The buckle had an *A* on it. "Adam," he said impulsively. His eyes fell on a Western picture by the door, and he added, "Russell."

"All right, Mr. Russell. We're through here." The doctor put the bandage in place and stepped back. "Now listen carefully. This is a watch, a chair and a table." He paused a minute. "Repeat what I said, please."

"Watch. Chair. Table."

The doctor took out an instrument and looked into each of Adam's eyes as he said, "Count by sevens for me, please."

Adam found he could, and for some reason this reassured him somewhat. He was even able to spell *world* backward when asked to do so.

"Now, what were those three words I said to you, and what day is it?"

"You said watch, chair, table, and today is Saturday."

"Very good." Dr. Kadlecek took a prescription pad out of his bag and gave it to Adam, along with a pen. "Draw me a picture of a star." When Adam was able to do so, the doctor said, "Very good. Now write a sentence. Just anything that comes to mind."

Adam wrote, "What is the lady's name?"

The doctor chuckled when he read it. "No sign of concussion or brain damage here." He gestured toward the woman. "This is Maya Kingsley, and you're on the Ranata ranch. Sound familiar?"

Adam slowly shook his head.

"Probably no reason it should. You must have been driving through and had an accident. I'll check into it. Meanwhile, I think you ought to stay put until at least tomorrow. Do you mind, Maya?"

"No, no. I insist upon it." Her voice was low and musical. "You lie down and get some rest. We'll find your car in the morning. The bathroom is through that door," she added. Then they left him alone.

As soon as the door closed behind them Maya asked, "Uncle Garth, is he badly hurt?"

"Not too badly. Exposure seems to be his worst problem. At first I was afraid of concussion, but he's alert and has good motor control. He passed the memory test. His pupils are the right size, and he seems to have no trouble focusing. The Babinski's reflex is absent. My guess is that he was in a wreck and that he's just shaken up."

"Dr. Kadlecek, you think it's okay for him to stay here?" Lupe asked in concern.

"Given the shape he's in, he won't feel up to any meanness for a while. I don't see any reason to rush him to the hospital. If Maya has no objection to a house guest, I suggest he stay here for a day or two or until we can locate his people."

"I have no objection. A guest is always welcome at the Ranata, especially one that looks as if he were run over by a team of mules."

Lupe gave her mistress a stubborn look. "I'll sleep here in the library. If he makes trouble, I'll get help."

"That's not necessary," Maya said with a smile. "Why, Javier practically had to carry him in. I doubt he'll be able to get out of bed tomorrow, much less tonight. Besides, all I have to do is press the alarm button anywhere in the house, and the men will come running."

Lupe looked unconvinced, but the doctor nodded. "I agree with Maya. Adam Russell won't do her any harm. Especially after that injection I gave him. You and Javier go on home."

Maya let them out and closed the door. Although she rarely bothered to lock it, leaving it unlocked tonight seemed especially wise. If the man did cause trouble, she wanted Javier and the others to be able to get in quickly. She walked back down the hallway and across the library to the guest room. Originally the library had been the common room, and the two rooms behind it had been the bedrooms. Now one was a den, and the other was reserved for guests.

As a child, Maya had often imagined she could hear the whispers of her long-vanished ancestors here and the sweep of their long skirts. Her fancy made her nervous again now as she pushed the guest-room door open and peeped in. There was something far more tangible than a ghost in the *hacienda* tonight. Until the others had gone, however, it hadn't occurred to her to think the stranger might really be dangerous.

The figure on the bed was motionless, so Maya crept silently into the room. Lupe had left on the small bedside lamp, which washed the man in a golden glow. He was handsome, no doubt about that, even with the faint bruise beneath his eye. His hair was Nordic blond, and his lean jaw hinted at a German ancestry. Other bruises marred the smooth skin of his bare torso. One arm lay across his stomach, and even in repose it looked powerful, with relaxed muscles and sinews, and prominent veins in his hand. The whiteness of the linen sheet contrasted sharply with the tan of his muscled frame. Rhythmically his chest rose and fell, and he made no move when Maya leaned over to look more closely at his face.

Satisfied that he was asleep, she gathered his clothes and unabashedly searched his pockets. They were empty. And he wasn't wearing a watch or a ring. The clothes were well made, and it struck her as odd that he wouldn't have at least a few coins or a driver's license. No one traveled this light. When she realized she was holding all his clothing and that that meant he must be nude beneath the sheet, she quickly backed out of the room.

She put his clothes in the washer and turned it on, still wondering why he had been traveling with no money and no identification. Had he been robbed? If so, why hadn't he mentioned it?

Leaving the clothes to wash, she retreated to her bedroom. The wall overlooking her private lagoon was glass, as were most of the other poolside walls. Since she lived alone, she seldom bothered to close the curtains, but she did so now. Even with the stranger unconscious, she felt his presence in the house.

Going to the large bathroom off her room, Maya slipped off her tunic and trousers and dropped them into the wicker hamper, along with her underwear. She showered and toweled dry, then crossed the thick honey-colored carpet of her bedroom to her closet.

Slipping into a nightgown in watery shades of pale blue, green and lavender, she went to her dresser and brushed her hair, which hung Indian-straight to below her waist. Once, years before, during a brief period of conformity in her life, she had cut it short and had hated it. Now it was again long and silky, and she made it a style of her own.

Her room, reflected in the dresser mirror, was decorated in the colors of the land she loved: muted, sunwashed hues combined with bleached white. Like all the rooms in the *hacienda*, her bedroom had a *kiva* fireplace, which was wonderfully cozy in the wintertime but served as a repository for potted plants the other nine months of the year. Her bedspread, a huge, brilliantly colored serape with knotted white string fringes, served as a focal point and lent the room a festive air. Maya curled up on it and gazed at the lazily circling ceiling fan. Who was this man she had so freely let into her house?

He had said his name was Adam Russell, but for some reason she wasn't so sure. Most people said their own names easily, but he had almost stammered it out. And he had no identification.

She knew she should be nervous, but somehow she was more intrigued.

Chapter Two

He slowly opened his eyes and blinked. This wasn't a room he knew, and he had a dizzying sensation of misplacement. The walls were white, and overhead were age-blackened beams and a ceiling fan. By shifting slightly he saw a rounded white adobe fireplace filled with geraniums, and in the niches above were colored candles of various sizes set in terra-cotta holders.

He rolled to his back and looked toward the sun-filled window, catching his breath when he discovered he wasn't alone. A woman stood there, her filmy garment billowing in the slight breeze. Her back was to him as she looked out the window. Her long hair was loose and as black as a raven's wing. She turned slightly, and the sunlight silhouetted her curvaceous body beneath the nearly transparent gown. He stared, deciding he had never seen anyone more lovely.

As if she felt his eyes upon her, she stepped away from the window, and the gown became a cover. She turned to look at him, and her eyes were startled. "I didn't know you were awake," she said. "I brought your clothes in."

He sat up, and at once his head began throbbing. He touched his forehead and found a bandage. "Where the hell am I?" he demanded. "Who are you?" Suddenly it dawned on him that he didn't know his own name, either.

"Don't you remember coming here? I'm Maya Kingsley. You're on the Ranata *rancho*."

Beneath the dull ache he began to recall the night before. "Yes. A doctor was here. He sewed up my head." But why had he needed stitches, and why the hell couldn't he remember his name?

"I washed your clothes and mended the shirt, Adam. I hope you don't mind."

He narrowed his eyes against the headache and studied her. Who was Adam? "Thank you," he said. He saw the Russell print on the wall and suddenly recalled telling them his name was Adam Russell, but he knew it wasn't. He just didn't know what it was. "Mrs. Kingsley, where..." He paused. There was no way he could frame all the questions that were crowding in on him.

"I'm not married. You may call me Maya. We aren't very formal around here."

He noticed his clothes folded neatly on the chair— *all* his clothes. He cocked his head to one side and looked at her questioningly.

"You undressed yourself," she explained quickly. "We are a bit more formal than that." She moved gracefully to the door, her sea-hued gown sweeping around her bare feet. "Lupe will have breakfast ready soon. Will you feel like joining us, or shall I have her bring it to you?"

"I'm a little stiff, but I think I'll be able to get up." He watched her leave and stared for a few minutes at the closed door. There was a sense of unreality about all of this, and it felt most unpleasant. He shoved back the sheet and slowly got out of bed. His muscles were sore, but he decided the exercise would loosen them up. The carpet was lush beneath his feet, and the room smelled of honeysuckle, as if there were a vine nearby. As he picked up his clothes he looked more closely at the picture on the wall. He was no longer sure it was a print. It looked like an original. He wondered how he knew that.

With a growl against his protesting body, he went into the bathroom and turned on the light—then came to a dead stop. The mirrored wall reflected a stranger with a bandage on his head. Slowly he went to the mirror and dropped his clothes on the blue-and-green tiled countertop. Leaning nearer, he studied his face as his panic began to grow again. He didn't have the least idea who he was, and, incredibly, he didn't even remember his own face! With sheer willpower he controlled himself, the effort making muscles tense in his reflected image. He could remember. He knew he could!

He hadn't forgotten everything. He knew, for instance, that this was amnesia. He knew he was in Texas, but not exactly which part of it. He clung to the things he knew and tried to remain rational about the things he didn't.

Suddenly he felt very vulnerable standing there naked, so he stepped into the hot shower and let the warmth and pulsing water soothe him. He dried himself quickly and dressed in the clothes the woman had left for him. Since he obviously was accustomed to shaving, and since there was a razor in the medicine cabinet, he shaved, then used the hair dryer to blow-dry his hair. Soon the image in the mirror looked more respectable—but not a bit more familiar.

He passed through the bedroom and found himself in a remarkably well-stocked library. Several over-stuffed chairs and a couch all covered in white duck were grouped around a colorful rug that appeared to have been hand-loomed. The inside wall was glass, affording a view of a patio and outdoor room. He saw Maya sitting under the shaded area as a Mexican woman served breakfast from a tray.

He stepped out and crossed the shady, cloisterlike walkway. Maya had changed into a peasant blouse and red skirt. Thin gold bracelets circled her wrist, and a narrow gold chain adorned her ankle. Her thick black hair was braided over one shoulder and tied with a red leather thong.

He sat opposite her across the white rattan table. Because he knew he had to say something, he ventured, "I hope I haven't been too much trouble."

"Not at all. How are you feeling?"

"As if a mule kicked me." He smiled his thanks as the maid put a plate of eggs and biscuits in front of him. "Where exactly am I?"

"In the back of nowhere," Maya replied with a smile. "The nearest town is La Avenida. It's about forty-five minutes from here. The nearest town of any *size* is San Antonio, about an hour and a half away." She pronounced it "San Antone." "What were you doing out here, anyway? Most people bypass us on the highways."

He shrugged and gave her what he hoped was a nonchalant grin. "Pass the salt and pepper?"

Maya studied him unabashedly while he seasoned his food. He didn't look like someone she should be wary of, yet she was almost agonizingly aware of him. He moved with a casual elegance totally unlike the rough gestures of her cowhands. "Are you from around here?"

"No," he guessed.

"I didn't think so. You don't look familiar, and I know most of the people in La Avenida."

"Have you lived here long?" He hoped to avoid her questions by asking some of his own. Perhaps one of her answers would trigger his memory.

"We've always been here," she said with pride. "My mother's family goes back to the Spanish occupation of the area during the 1700s. My father's people had settled here before Moses Austin decided to colonize Texas. The Ranata is one of the original Spanish land grants."

He gazed at her across the table. Even in the morning light she was flawlessly beautiful. Her eyes were not brown as he had expected, but gray—actually more a silver with an ebony rim that made them sensuously smoky. Her skin was a pale gold tan and looked as soft as a flower petal. Realizing he was staring, he turned his attention to his breakfast.

"Why don't you have any identification on you?" she asked unexpectedly.

When he looked up sharply, she said quickly, "I had to go through your pockets so I could wash your clothes."

"I like to travel light." Why *was* he here? he wondered. This wasn't the sort of place he could have stumbled onto easily.

She looked unconvinced, but she finished her eggs and leaned back in her chair to sip her coffee. Over the rim of her cup, she watched him. He certainly didn't act or speak in the manner of a penniless drifter. "What sort of work do you do?"

"Oh, this and that." He looked over at the sunlit pool. "It's going to be a hot one."

"In Texas all days are hot in July." She narrowed her eyes thoughtfully. Adam's virility drew her like a magnet. His eyes met hers unexpectedly, and she glanced away. "If your sunburn is bothering you, we have some aloe vera growing in the side garden. There's nothing better for a burn. Just rub the pulp over your skin."

"It's not bothering me." The day was already hot, but Maya looked as cool as if she had her own personal breeze. Under other circumstances he knew he'd be bending over backward to get to know her better. Or would he? For all he knew, he had a wife and even children somewhere. The idea made him frown. Was someone worried about him? If so, why couldn't he remember who? "You have quite a library," he said to keep his thoughts calm.

"There isn't much out here for entertainment at night except television and books. I prefer to read. My father was a doctor, so some are his medical books."

"Oh?" he said with interest. Medical texts would have information on amnesia.

"He and Uncle Garth had a practice in La Avenida. He's not my real uncle, but I've known him all my life. When he retired, Dad talked him into moving out here, since he has no family. Now that Dad is gone, Uncle Garth takes care of the workers and helps Javier doctor the animals." She let her voice trail away under Adam's intense stare. His moss-green eyes were so compelling that she kept losing her train of thought.

"Do you mind if I look through a couple of books before I go?" He wondered where he was supposed to go when he had no idea where he was from, but he couldn't camp in her spare room forever.

"I don't mind at all, but how do you expect to leave? I sent the men out to the road, and there's no sign of your car."

"No?"

"There's no report of a wreck, either. I phoned the sheriff in La Avenida to ask. There were no reports of any abandoned vehicle."

Adam looked away and got hastily to his feet as if intrigued by the pool's waterfall. No car? Then how had he gotten here? He walked across tiles to the pool and gazed down into the jade water. He couldn't have just dropped in here from nowhere!

Maya wandered out to stand beside him. In the sunlight her hair had bluish highlights and her eyes were a mercurial gray. "If you want to call someone to come get you, there's a phone in the living room." She was surprisingly hesitant to tell him that. For some reason she wasn't looking forward to his departure.

"That's not necessary," he said brusquely.

"Which way were you coming when you had the accident? Maybe your car hasn't been found because it ran off the road into a gully."

"I'm not sure. It was dark."

Again she looked at him thoughtfully. "Are you married?"

"No." The word slipped out easily, and he wondered if that meant it was the truth. Certainly he didn't feel married. As a matter of fact, now that he was full and rested, he was acutely aware of Maya by his side.

"Well, if no one is waiting for you, there's no reason for you to be in a hurry to leave," she heard herself saying. "I mean, without a car, how could you get to wherever you're going?" She moistened her lips and looked up at him. "Where *are* you going?"

"No place in particular, I guess."

His eyes seemed to probe her very soul, as if he were searching for something, but then he looked away.

"Besides, you have some rather extensive bruises. Uncle Garth is going to want to keep an eye on you for at least a few days."

"We wouldn't want to make it hard on Uncle Garth," he said with forced lightness.

"On the other hand, we aren't holding you prisoner here. If you want to leave, no one will stop you."

"I can't think of a single place I'd rather be just at the moment," he said wryly. When she looked puzzled he added, "But I won't impose on you for long. I'll be on my way as soon as my car is found."

She strolled with him back to the shady chairs as Lupe cleared away the breakfast dishes. "Where did you work last?"

"I beg your pardon?"

"You said you do this and that. I assume you're a drifter?" She waited for him to deny it.

"I guess you could say that."

"So where did you work last?"

"Down the road a ways," he replied, waving vaguely toward the east. "I forget their name."

"Hmm," she replied doubtfully. "Was it Cooper?"

"Yeah. That was it."

She nodded. "They hire a lot of people for branding."

He smiled as if agreeing with her. Because Maya's voice sounded unaccented to his ear, he assumed he, too, was from Texas. San Antonio, perhaps? It didn't seem familiar, but then, neither did anything else.

"Will you excuse me for a minute? If you want to look at the books, just make yourself at home." She gave him a disarming smile and went into the living room.

From there she surreptitiously watched Adam walk quickly back to the library and start to scan the row of books. He seemed to be looking for something in particular.

With a slight frown, Maya went to the phone and punched in the Coopers' number. "Shelley? I'm sorry to bother you so early." She paused and glanced down the hall to be sure her guest was well out of hearing. "There's a man here who says he worked for you at branding. Adam Russell. No? Will you check with Ed?" She waited impatiently while Shelley asked her husband. Even before her friend returned to the phone, Maya knew the answer. "Ed says he never heard of him?" She gave a short laugh. "Well, so much for references. No, no. Everything is fine. I'll talk to you later. Bye."

Maya hung up and stood indecisively as her apprehension grew. To have let an injured stranger sleep in her guest room was one thing, but he was wide-awake now, and most of her men were out doing their chores. Lupe would be of little help if Adam suddenly revealed himself to be dangerous.

Carefully she drew in a deep breath to calm herself. He might have lied about working for the Coopers, but he had given her no other reason for alarm. If he had violence or robbery on his mind, surely he would have tried something earlier.

On the other hand, she thought, he must have a terrific headache from that cut and a lot of sore muscles from those bruises. Besides, he had no identification at all. What sort of person wandered in off the back roads with nothing at all in his pockets? True, he was handsome, but where was it written that all dangerous people were ugly? He spoke as if he were well educated, but maybe he had completed college before he took up a life of mayhem.

With an effort she slowed herself down. She had always had an overactive imagination, and it was merely running away with her again. There must be a perfectly reasonable explanation for his stumbling onto her doorstep in the middle of the night, claiming he had been in an accident when there was no sign of one anywhere around.

She went down the long hall and stood in the library doorway for a moment to watch him. He had evidently found what he was looking for because he was poring over a book, one of her father's medical texts. He looked up in surprise as he became aware of her presence.

"Did you find something interesting?" she asked lightly as she crossed the room. "*Taber's Cyclopedic Medical Dictionary*. An unusual choice of reading material."

He snapped the volume shut. "It just happened to catch my eye."

"Are you sure it was the Coopers you worked for?"

"Positive."

"That's strange. I just talked to Shelley Cooper, and neither she nor Ed ever heard of you."

"It must have been some other Cooper," he said with a shrug as he replaced the book.

"There *are* no other Coopers," she said with a flash of temper. "Now, suppose you tell me the truth. Who are you, and why are you here?"

"Calm down. I don't mean you any harm."

"No? Why should I believe that?"

He stepped nearer. "Lower your voice before you have everyone running in here to see what's wrong."

She knew all too well how soundproof the *hacienda* was. Even a shout wouldn't alert Lupe back in the kitchen, and she was nowhere near the alarm button. She eased past him toward the alarm. "Then tell me what you're doing here," she bluffed.

Suddenly his hands shot out and he braced himself against the bookshelves, trapping her between his arms. "I said lower your voice!"

At that moment Maya couldn't have made a sound if her life depended on it, and she wondered frantically if it did.

He looked down at her and saw the fluttering pulse in her throat. She didn't cower away from him, but fear was evident in her eyes. He dropped his arms. "I didn't mean to scare you."

"Me? Afraid? Why should I be afraid?" She slid nearer the button. Once she was close enough, she lunged to press it, but before she could reach it, he caught her wrist. Her eyes widened in terror.

"Don't do that," he said in a low voice. "Please."

Perhaps it was the "please" that reassured her, or maybe the fact that he held her firmly but not painfully. Maya quit struggling and drew back.

He led her to the couch and pulled her down to sit beside him. Only then did he release her arm. "I can explain all this."

"You said you were in a wreck. What kind of car were you driving? Where were you going that would put you on this road?" Her suspicion was making her questions come out in a rush.

"I don't know."

She tried to bolt up from the couch, but he caught her around the waist and yanked her back. "Will you be still and listen to me?" he demanded. He leaned over her, imprisoning her against the soft cushions.

"What reason could you possibly have for refusing to answer me?" she demanded.

"I didn't refuse. I really don't know." She tried to squirm free, but he held her firmly. "I have amnesia."

"What? That's the most ridiculous thing I ever heard of! Turn me loose!"

"Not until you listen to me. I lied about working for the Coopers, and I may have lied about being in a wreck. I assumed that's what happened, but I don't remember."

"How could you not remember? And how did you know the Coopers' name?"

"I didn't. You supplied that."

She frowned as she tried to remember.

"As I recall, Dr. Kadlecek was the one who said I had been in an accident in the first place."

"Well, if you weren't in a wreck, then where did you get those bruises and that cut?"

"I told you, I don't know."

"You must remember something! You know your name, and I always thought—"

"I made it up," he interrupted. "I'm telling you I don't remember anything prior to sitting in that bedroom last night. I don't even know how I got here."

Maya forgot her own fear long enough to see the fear buried in his eyes, and she stopped trying to escape. "You really don't know who you are?" she asked softly.

He heard the change in her voice, and warily he released her. "No, I don't."

She slowly sat up and readjusted her blouse, which had slid down over her shoulder. "Why should I believe you this time when you lied before?"

"I lied because I was afraid. Do you have any idea what it's like not to know who you are? I don't have any idea how I got here or even why I was passing through!"

"If you ask me, that would be more than enough reason to admit it right out, not to lie about it!"

"Don't take my word for it. There are the medical books. Look it up for yourself. Lying to try to establish normalcy is a common way of trying to cope with amnesia. It says so in the book."

Maya still looked doubtful but no longer filled with fear. He said more gently, "I'm sorry I frightened you, but I couldn't let you sound the alarm without giving me a chance to explain."

"How did you know that button would sound an alarm?"

"It doesn't seem reasonable that you would be fighting so hard to turn on a light switch, now, does it? I'm suffering from amnesia, not stupidity." He saw her rub her wrist and added, "Did I hurt you?" He reached out and took her hand to examine her wrist.

When his hand touched hers, she felt a tingling sensation race all the way to her heart. "I'm...I'm all right." She tried to withdraw her hand, but he held it tenderly and clearly did not want to release it. Their eyes met, and she felt mesmerized by the intense longing she saw there.

Both hurriedly drew back. He glanced at her as if he, too, had felt that incredible sensation. Then he shook his head as if to deny it. "Do you believe me?"

"I don't know. I mean, it's pretty incredible."

"I know. If I were in your place, I wouldn't believe it for a minute. Still it's true." He rested his forearms on his knees and tilted his head to study her. "If you want me to, I'll go. Just tell me where the nearest town is."

"I can't just point you toward town and send you off if you really do have amnesia!" She frowned at him. "You must have *some* idea who you are or where you came from."

"I think I'm from Texas. Our accents are very similar."

"But not identical. At any rate, you aren't from around here, or I'd know you."

He shrugged.

"What do you do for a living?"

"How should I know? I don't even know my name," he said in exasperation.

She took his hand and turned it palm up. "You aren't a cowboy. There aren't any calluses."

"Maybe I don't work at all?"

She ignored the comment. "You must work inside or you wouldn't have sunburned so badly. Besides, you talk as if you have an education.'' She ran her fingers over the pads of his hands. The skin was hard but not as rough as it would have been if he worked out in the elements. Then the unconscious sensuousness of the gesture took her by surprise, and she looked up to find him watching her closely. His gaze was intense, as if he were feeling some strong emotion. Hastily she released his hand. ''No, you're not a laborer.''

He had been startled at the way Maya's hand felt on his. He could still feel the soft imprint of her fingertips trailing across his palm. Her touch seemed to crack a barrier deep inside him. Why, he wondered, would he think that?

''You seemed to know where to look in the medical books. Maybe you're a doctor.''

''I think it's more likely I can figure out how to look up the word *amnesia*. The jargon was understandable but not familiar.''

She stared at him. ''Why did you say your name was Adam Russell?''

''My belt buckle has an *A* on it. I took the last name from the picture hanging on the wall.''

''Oh.''

Her troubled eyes searched his, and he wondered if she believed him or if she was merely humoring him until she could summon help.

''Adam was the first name to pop into my mind. It doesn't feel any more familiar than Andy or Allan or Alphonso.''

She smiled slightly. ''My guess is that it isn't Alphonso.''

''I hope not,'' he said with an answering smile.

"Well, if you have no idea who you are or where you're going, you can't very well leave." She was surprised to find how pleased she was at the idea of having him around for a while longer.

"I can't stay in your guest room indefinitely."

"I'm sure someone is combing the bushes for you. Certainly you don't look like someone who would be easily misplaced." Her words made her blush, and she stood up quickly. "I'll contact the sheriff in La Avenida and see if there is a missing-persons report for someone of your description. In the meantime, I think Uncle Garth should check you more closely and be sure you don't have a worse head injury than we think."

He stood also and gazed down at her. Although he didn't touch her, she had the curious feeling of being caressed.

"Thank you," he said softly.

Maya didn't quite trust herself to answer. Already she knew what Uncle Garth would say about her letting "Adam" stay at the Ranata.

Chapter Three

What you have is retrograde amnesia," Garth said as Adam buttoned his shirt. "I've never seen a case where the patient lost more than a day or so, usually only hours. Most times we see it in football injuries—things like that."

"How long does it last?"

"Hard to say. You probably won't ever recall the injury itself or what immediately preceded it. The rest will likely come back in bits and pieces."

Maya looked at Adam. "Surely there's something we can do to trigger his memory."

The doctor shrugged. "I don't know of any way to rush it along. Like I say, I've never seen anyone lose so much of his past. In the injuries I've treated it's returned pretty fast, but then again, not so much was gone. I'd say it's a sure thing, though, that it's the result of the injury to your head and not due to illness."

"Then I may not have been in a car wreck at all."

"Son, from the way you're bruised, I'd say a fight was more likely. Now, where you found somebody to fight with out here, I can't say."

Adam rubbed the bruises on his stomach. "You're probably right about the fight. Funny, I don't feel like someone who would get into brawls." He frowned. "Maybe I'm not myself at all. Can a person's personality be altered by amnesia?"

"I'm no psychiatrist, but I guess anything is possible." He fastened his medical bag and said, "Other than that, you seem to be recovering quite well. There's still no sign of internal injuries, and there's no reason to think you'll have trouble other than this loss of memory."

"That's all?" Adam asked wryly. "That seems to be enough."

"Could be worse. You found the Ranata. Otherwise you might have died of exposure or thirst. You have no internal injuries or broken bones. Count yourself lucky." The doctor picked up his bag and said, "I've got to go over to the Salazars'. Rosa is expecting any time now, and I'm keeping a close eye on her." He nodded to Adam. "Take it easy."

When he was gone, Adam said, "Does he know what he's talking about?"

"Don't let Uncle Garth's down-home manner fool you. He's very good."

Adam tucked in his shirttail and paced the guest bedroom. "What the hell am I supposed to do? I can't impose on your hospitality indefinitely, and I don't know where else to go or how to earn a living." The admission embarrassed him, and he ran his fingers through his hair in exasperation.

"You aren't imposing. I'd be glad to have you stay." Maya moved uneasily and added, "I didn't mean that to sound as if I were, well, suggesting anything improper. Only that the house is big, and I don't object to your being here." She pointed toward the ceiling. "There are two suites of rooms upstairs that haven't been used since my parents died, as well as a study and sewing room." He was gazing at her as if he could see past her facade and into the loneliness that plagued her nights. "You won't bother me at all," she finished lamely. What was there about him that blasted through her customary defense system of aloofness?

"Maybe I could work around here and earn my keep for a week or two. Surely by then I'll be back to normal."

"Judging by your hands and speech, you don't know the first thing about ranching. Can you speak Spanish?"

"I don't think so."

"Most of the hands speak no English. I think it's a better idea if you concentrate on finding out who you are." She went to the phone and dialed a number.

Adam listened in surprise as she casually called a store in La Avenida and told them to send out several changes of clothes in his sizes. When she hung up, he said, "Do you do that sort of thing often? Call up a store and order wardrobes for strange men?"

Maya lifted her head regally. "No, but no one will question it. I'm Maya Kingsley, and this is the Ranata. The clothes will arrive within the hour."

"I can't accept this from you!"

"What choice do you have? You can't run around naked while those clothes are being washed." She struggled not to blush at the visual image of his muscular torso and how the sheet had ridden low around his waist the night before as she watched him sleep. "I know in novels there are always clothes left by a father or brother, but I have no brother, and I got rid of Dad's clothes after he died. Besides, he outweighed you by twenty pounds, and his taste left a lot to be desired."

"I have no way of paying for them," Adam pointed out stubbornly. "I may have amnesia, but I know I'm no gigolo."

"From all I've heard, gigolos do quite a bit to earn their favors." The blush overtook her, and she looked away. "I didn't mean to imply..."

"I know you didn't."

"If you want me to, I'll call and cancel the order."

Adam sighed and shook his head. "As you've pointed out, I have to have clothes. I'll pay you back when I get all this worked out."

"There's one other call I ought to make. I should contact the sheriff and see if there's anything new about an accident or a missing person."

"Yes. You should do that."

Again Maya dialed a number. "Hello, Joe Bob? This is Maya Kingsley again. Any reports yet on that description I gave you?" She looked across the room at Adam. "Yes, he's still here. Of course you're welcome to come out and see him. All right. I'll see you soon." She hung up. "Joe Bob wants to come see you. There's a report out for someone about your size and coloring."

"Why are you frowning?"

"He didn't say it was for a missing person, and from the way he was hedging, I think he meant a criminal description."

"I never thought of that!"

"Then you must have nothing to worry about. I mean, if you were a bank robber or something, surely you'd have an instinctive fear of my calling a sheriff."

Adam didn't look convinced. "I don't even have an instinctive feel for my own name, much less for what I may have done."

Sheriff Joe Bob Walters arrived within a half hour. He rigorously enforced the speed limit for others but had no qualms about exceeding it himself. As the pale gold dust settled over the private road and his shiny patrol car, he knocked loudly on the wooden door.

Maya opened it and said, "Come in, Joe Bob. Adam's out on the patio."

Joe Bob pulled out a white handkerchief and wiped the sweat from his jowly red face. His pale hazel eyes squinted at the man through the glass wall, and he breathed as laboriously as if he had run all the way from town. "It's gonna be a hot one." As he nodded toward the stranger, he said to her, "He made any suspicious moves yet?"

"Of course not. Come out and meet him." Though she had known him all her life, Maya sometimes found Joe Bob very exasperating. She preceded him through the open door and said, "Adam, this is our sheriff, Joe Bob Walters. Joe Bob, this is Adam Russell."

"Russell?"

"It seemed to be as good a name as any." Adam held out his hand to the sheriff. "Maya said you might have a lead on who I really am."

"Yeah," Joe Bob said with a show of reluctance as he eased himself down onto a chair that creaked under his bulk. He fished a paper from his back pocket and consulted it, then looked at Adam.

Maya folded her arms and leaned against a column. "Well? Is this the man?"

"It says here his eyes are supposed to be blue, but that don't mean much. Sometimes eyes look different in one light or another. Roll up your sleeves, please, sir. Let me see your upper arms."

Slowly Adam shoved up the sleeves that were folded back to bare his forearms. He showed both arms to the sheriff.

"Says this man has a tattoo of a snake on one arm and a swastika on the other. I don't reckon you're him," he concluded with a shake of his head. "In a way, I wish you was. This here man's wanted in three states. Armed robbery."

"Frankly, I'm glad to disappoint you," Adam said.

"Aren't there any reports of missing people?" Maya asked. "Surely somebody would notice he's gone."

"If he's only been gone a day, no one would file a report yet," Joe Bob explained as he carefully folded the paper and returned it to his pocket. "If he's a drifter, there might not be anybody to know he's lost."

"Does he look like a drifter to you?" she demanded. "Listen to the way he talks."

"Can't go by that. Some bums talk as good as me. Still bums, though." He watched Adam as if he were a specimen on a slide. "These days you can't tell the good boys from the bad." He heaved himself to his feet and studied Adam as he, too, rose. "Got any scars or tattoos at all?"

"No," Maya said before she thought.

Adam raised his eyebrows in amusement before saying, "Not one, sheriff."

Joe Bob paused as if he were considering this. "Want to get a ride into town with me? I'm going straight back."

"No, I'm staying here."

"Here?" Joe Bob pointed down at the tiled floor. "At the Ranata?"

"That's right," Maya agreed. "That seems to be the most reasonable solution. He has no money for a room in town, and I have plenty of space here."

The sheriff's brows met over the bridge of his short nose, and he said, "Maya, you can't do that."

She laughed in amazement. No one ever told her she could or couldn't do anything. "Yes, I can."

"I assure you, sheriff, I mean no harm. I've offered to work for my keep."

"You'll be staying out in one of the *casitas*, then?" Joe Bob said with relief.

"That's none of your business," Maya said coolly. "I only want you to find out who he is, not chaperone me."

Joe Bob frowned from one to the other, but in a polite tone he said, "Maya, walk out to the car with me." He took her arm and propelled her out the door. When they were alone he said, "Are you crazy? You can't stay out here all by yourself with this man!"

"The Ranata is full of people, and you know it," she countered. "We're hardly alone. Lupe is in the kitchen, some of the men are always within sight of the house, and you know about my alarm system." She tried not to recall how effectively Adam had prevented her from using it earlier. "I'm perfectly safe."

"But think how it will look to folks, even if he *isn't* up to no good!"

"I've never especially worried about public opinion, Joe Bob. I tend my fences and expect everyone else to tend theirs."

"Maya, dang it, he may be a criminal! You could get your throat cut before you could call for help."

"If that were true, he would have done it already, or at least acted suspiciously."

Joe Bob shook his large head. "I don't believe this stuff about amnesia. It sounds phony to me. If you ask me, he's a con man."

"A what?" she asked in disbelief.

"What better way to weasel himself into the Ranata than to play on your sympathy? You're a rich woman, Maya, and everybody knows it."

"Do you think he also beat himself up? No, Joe Bob. You'll have to do better than that."

"Okay. Can't nobody tell you nothing. Never could. But if you wake up with your throat cut, don't blame me for not trying to talk sense into you."

"I'll keep that in mind."

She watched the sheriff get into his car and drive away at the head of a small dust storm. Was she really so sure this stranger meant her no harm? She had no reason to trust him except that he had not yet hurt her. Good looks and articulateness didn't necessarily mean a thing.

She went back into the cavelike coolness of the house. Adam stood by the pool, gazing down at the water. Slowly she closed the outside door and leaned against the thick wood. Was she so lonely that any stranger could move into her house and she'd welcome him with open arms? She didn't like the idea. She prided herself on her fierce independence.

As if he felt her eyes on him, he turned and gazed at her. She walked out to stand beside him in the hot sunlight. Even though she was tall, she had to tilt her head back to look into his eyes.

"Did he warn you against me?" Adam asked.

"Naturally."

"Maybe he's right. You know nothing about me at all."

"Joe Bob is good for keeping vandals under control and for catching an occasional cattle rustler, but he's not an expert on whom I should trust."

"Cattle rustlers? I thought those went out with Jesse James."

"We get a few now and then. These days they use trucks."

He studied her as if he wasn't too sure what to think of her. "You're not afraid of me?"

"I've rarely been afraid in my entire life."

"Most women would be if they lived way out here alone."

"The Ranata isn't just my home," she explained, "it's me. It's in my blood and bones. I guess you couldn't understand what that means unless your family had been on the same land for more generations than you could count. Nothing can hurt me here because I belong here."

"Having a couple dozen hired hands around for protection doesn't hurt, either."

She gave him her mystically knowing smile and let him believe as he pleased. Glancing up at the sky, she said, "Ever hear the saying that no one goes out in the midday sun except mad dogs and Englishmen? Maybe we should search for your identity farther afield.''

''With this accent?'' He laughed. ''Not likely.'' They strolled back to the shade of the patio roof. ''Tell me more about these cattle rustlers. I'm intrigued.''

''Sometimes they'll steal a prize bull and use him to service a herd, then either sell him across the border or simply turn him loose to be found. Last year someone stole my best bull and hamstrung him to make him more manageable. When they dumped him back in the pasture, his back legs were crippled.'' Anger over the needless cruelty sharpened her voice.

''Did you have to destroy him?''

''No, Javier came up with a really brilliant idea. He thought the legs would heal if we could keep the bull's weight off them. You haven't seen my cattle, but I raise Charolais, and they're huge; this bull had to be hauled in a four-horse trailer. Well, there weren't any trees in the pasture or feedlot that were large enough to support him, so Javier dug a trench and suspended the bull from an A-frame hoist they use to pull engines out of cars. Not only did it keep the bull off his injured legs until they could heal, but it kept him immobile for the men to doctor him. That bull had a mean temper to start with, and Javier found it a little difficult to turn him loose again when the time came.'' She laughed at the memory. ''That's one mean bull, and he didn't mellow a bit from being confined.''

''You have a beautiful smile,'' Adam said.

Maya's eyes widened, and she lost her train of thought. His moss-hued gaze seemed to probe her innermost secrets, and she found that feeling both exciting and disturbing. Amusement flickered in the depths of his eyes as he said, "How do you know I don't have any scars or tattoos?"

Maya stood abruptly. "Would you like some lemonade? Lupe makes it fresh, and there's none better anywhere."

"Lemonade? Why not?"

She hurried through the dining room and into the kitchen, but even putting distance between them didn't calm the racing of her pulse. The kitchen, originally a building separate from the *hacienda*, was now incorporated into the sprawling house. Long strings of red peppers and jars of *jalapeños* lined the rafters and shelves, and dried herbs from Lupe's garden hung from pegs on the wall. The huge fireplace was rarely used except for large-scale barbecues, since the latest in kitchen equipment had been installed. The countertops were vivid blue, yellow and white Mexican tiles, and the floor was made of quarry tile that had been baked in the backyard a hundred years before.

Maya asked Lupe in rapid Spanish for two glasses of lemonade and tried to calm herself while she waited. She was lonely and he was handsome and that's all there was to it. Unfortunately, she knew she was lying to herself. Adam wasn't the only handsome man she knew, and he certainly wasn't the only one to show interest in her. Maya was single by choice, not due to lack of proposals.

As she waited there was a knock on the back door. It was the delivery man from the clothing store in La Avenida. When she took the package from him, Lupe looked at her disapprovingly but didn't speak. Maya said simply, "He has to have clothes to wear."

"*Sí,*" the older woman said flatly.

Maya sighed. She had never understood how Lupe could put so much innuendo into one syllable. "Well, he does."

Lupe gave her the two glasses on a tray and took the package. "I'll put these in the *señor*'s room." Her tightened lips registered disapproval.

Maya wondered why Joe Bob thought she was unchaperoned. Between Lupe, Javier and Uncle Garth, she had more people watching her than she wanted or needed. She carried the lemonade back to Adam and put it on the table. "Your clothes have arrived. Would you like to go for a swim?"

"Sure. If you are."

She hadn't planned to, but she found herself nodding. "I'll go change." She crossed the sunlit patio to her room and felt his disquieting gaze upon her all the way. Refusing to look back, she slipped into the shadowy recess of her room and slid the glass door shut. Peeping between the curtains, she saw that Adam was no longer on the patio after all. Feeling foolish, she crossed the room and pulled open the drawer where she kept her swimsuits. Why did she feel vaguely perturbed that he hadn't been watching her? she wondered.

She pushed aside her bikinis. Even though she was proud of her figure, she felt the need for a more effective cover-up. She pulled on a bright red one-piece and tossed it onto the bed. She knew she was being silly to feel so nervous about swimming in her own pool, but she was, nevertheless.

She undressed and smoothed the swimsuit on. It was cut low in the back and high on the sides, and the front allowed a generous amount of cleavage to show.

Even if it was her most decorous suit, it wasn't prim by any means.

In the bathroom she twisted her hair into a sleek bun high on her crown. She seldom let it get wet when she swam because all that hair was so heavy. The rather severe style gave her the aspect of a ballerina, she decided. Good. Ballerinas usually didn't exude sensuality. Of course, she thought as she surveyed herself in the mirror, they didn't usually sport that much cleavage, either. She futilely tugged at the top of her suit, but it wouldn't rise any higher.

"You're being so silly," she muttered to her reflection. Adam probably wouldn't care one way or another how she looked.

He was already on the patio when she stepped out of her room, and his expression told her he definitely did care. She hesitated, then dived into the pool. The cool water closed over her head and temporarily put her in another world, but she couldn't stay submerged forever. She swam to the surface and clung to the rim of the pool. So much for keeping her hair dry, she thought.

Adam came to the edge of the pool and tossed his towel onto a canvas chair. His body was lean and as graceful as a panther's, Maya noted appreciatively. The swimsuit she had ordered fit as if it were made for him.

He smiled as he looked down at her. "I've always liked red." Effortlessly he dived into the water, scarcely making a splash.

When he bobbed up, she said, "How do you know? Is that a memory?"

"I think it's that suit." He grinned at her, his white teeth flashing in his sunburned face.

"You should stay out of the sun or you'll get a worse burn," she said sharply to hide her quickening response.

His grin broadened as if he knew exactly what she was feeling. "I'll be careful."

She pushed away and swam a lap, her long, clean strokes pulling her swiftly through the water. The pool often provided her with a temporary escape from her problems. This problem, however, was keeping perfect pace with her, his strokes as sure as her own.

When she was out of breath, she paused at the deep end and said, "You've obviously done quite a bit of swimming."

"Maybe I'm an itinerant lifeguard."

She laughed. "No doubt. You're swimming your way across the state, stopping to save lives whenever you need the cash. A true knight-errant."

He surprised her by reaching up and touching her damp cheek. "You really are beautiful. Even soaking wet."

Maya wanted to pull away, yet at the same time she wanted to swim closer. The water enfolding them both made the touch more intimate, as if sharing the same element made them one. Because of the aridness of the land she loved, water was more sensuous to her than she cared to admit. Swimming with Adam was almost a sexual experience.

His fingers caressed the graceful curve of her neck and stopped on her fluttering pulse. Although his lips tilted up slightly to make light of the moment, his eyes were serious as they read the message in hers. She forced herself to look away, but her gaze magnetically returned to meet his.

"Are you frightened?" he asked gently as he gauged the beating of her heart.

"No." Her voice sounded breathless, even to herself, and she knew it had nothing to do with the swim. "Are you?"

"Lady, you scare me half to death."

Her eyes widened in surprise, but he swam away without explaining.

After a few more laps they waded out of the shallow end and climbed the rock steps. He startled her by rubbing her back dry with his towel, then turning her to dry her face and throat. As the towel blotted the water from her chest and the exposed tops of her breasts, she felt the breath catch in her throat. His eyes followed the towel admiringly, then met her gaze.

"For a man who's scared half to death, you sure like to live dangerously," she observed.

"Does that mean there's someone else who usually dries you off after a swim?" He seemed intent as he waited for her answer.

"I usually let the sun dry me."

"Then there isn't a man in your life?"

"Not an important one. I have friends, but they're only that. I have no lover, and I'm not engaged."

"And you're very direct."

"The question seemed to warrant directness."

For a moment she thought he was about to kiss her, but he pulled back. Disappointment coursed through her. "Our lemonade," he said. "Remember?"

Most of the ice had melted, but even diluted, Lupe's lemonade was a treat. The noonday sun beat down on the patio, and even the shaded area was hot. Maya rolled the frosty glass over her forehead and cheeks and closed her eyes. As much as she loved the heat, by July she yearned for the respite of autumn.

She opened her eyes to find Adam watching her. Hastily she took a sip of lemonade.

He smiled lazily. "Lucky glass."

She glanced at him sharply, but he had looked away.

"I think we should try to jog my memory," he said conversationally. "We must be able to think of some way to make my brain work right." He rubbed his temple and added, "It's all in there. All my past and my identity. I just need to access it." When Maya remained silent, he glanced at her. "Why are you looking at me like that?"

"You said 'access it.' That's a term used by people who work with computers."

He leaned forward and put his glass on the table. "Computer," he said thoughtfully. "I seem to see one, but it may be simply because I know what computers are. I think I could use one, though. That's not much to go on. Virtually every profession uses computers these days."

"Exactly. The *professions* do. That tallies with your hands being smooth. It's something to work with, even if it's not much."

"I guess at this point everything counts." He looked at her for a moment, then said, "I have a feeling that, before much longer, it's going to be very important for me to know who I am. You know there's no man in your life, but I..." He hesitated, disturbed by the thought, then plunged on. "I don't know if I have someone waiting for me."

"Do you think you do?" she asked quietly.

He shook his head. "If I were in love with a woman, I think I'd know it."

"You could have commitments and not have love. It happens."

"Maybe." He spread his left hand. "There's no light mark as if I were used to wearing a wedding band."

"Not all married men wear them."

"That's true. If I had someone, though, why would I be wandering around alone? I wouldn't leave my woman behind, no matter how badly I had been hurt. And I'd fight to the death before I'd let her be taken from me." Surprised at his own impassioned argument, he took a deep breath, then continued more calmly. "No I must have been alone. Separate vacations doesn't sound like a couple in love."

"Not all couples are, but they're still couples."

He leaned back in the chair and gazed out at the sun-drenched tiles. "If I had a wife or fiancée, I'd know it. I'm certain of it."

Maya didn't dispute his word, though she wondered if he could really be so sure. Once, years before, a man had sworn he loved her. He had professed undying love in the most tender of terms. Resolutely Maya put him out of her thoughts as she always did. But she still wasn't convinced that men were as constant in their love as Adam seemed to believe.

She looked sideways at him from beneath her long eyelashes. On the other hand, if she were in love with a man, really in love, she didn't think she would ever forget him. Not completely. Not if it were a man like Adam.

The track of her thoughts startled her, and she looked away quickly. She didn't even know him! Not really. But somewhere deep inside, with an elemental part of herself, she knew that she did. Maybe not in this lifetime, maybe not in this guise, but she knew him. She had known him all along.

Keeping her face carefully blank, she sipped her lemonade and was grateful that he couldn't hear her thoughts. She wished *she* could be as impervious to them.

Adam looked over at her and smiled.

Chapter Four

Adam tossed aside the atlas and frowned. "It's useless. All of Texas is familiar to me. So are parts of Louisiana and Colorado. Assuming I know Colorado from past vacations and that I know Louisiana because it's so close, that still doesn't tell me anything."

"Maybe it does. You must be from a town closer to Louisiana than Oklahoma or New Mexico. That cuts out a lot of territory."

"And puts us in the most densely populated part of the state." He stood, paced to the window and gazed out over the sun-baked grass and mesquite trees. "It's like looking for a needle in a haystack when you've never even seen a needle."

Maya went to him and put a hand on his arm. "Don't be discouraged. Uncle Garth said it may take time. We've only been trying for three days."

He smiled mirthlessly. "To you it's three days. To me it's my whole lifetime." He let his gaze travel to the rolling hills in the distance. Barely visible in the rippling yellow grass and jutting rock, four deer grazed without fear. "I find myself lying awake at night and repeating the day's events. It's as if I might lose them if I don't check them over and over. I find myself making up histories for myself in hopes something will seem familiar and trigger a real memory." He looked back at her. "At times I'm even afraid of going crazy."

"Don't be. Uncle Garth said you're in no danger of anything like that. This is the result of an injury. You won't lose what you have now. It doesn't work that way."

"I still worry. I feel as if I'm in one of those nightmares where you try to get somewhere but you can never quite make it."

"I'm sorry, Adam. I know it must be terrible for you." Her gray eyes were troubled as she looked up at him.

Adam wondered if Maya had any idea how much she figured in his new memories. Each night he recalled her gestures, the pitch of her voice, every word and phrase. He dwelt on her provocative red swimsuit and the way the hot breezes pushed her silky garments against her delectable body. He had been drawn to her from the very beginning, but now his thoughts were taking a decidedly erotic turn. He dreamed of her lying beneath him in bed while he loved her with an all-consuming passion.

He watched as she picked up the atlas and flipped through the pages. She seemed so self-assured, so tranquil. Did she have dreams of passion? he wondered. Did she ever ache for the touch of a lover's hands? At times he thought he caught glimpses of veiled desire in her smoky eyes, but she never gave him a clue as to whether she would welcome an advance from him. One thing was certain: she wasn't a woman to indulge in a careless affair. He knew without a doubt that Maya Kingsley would have to care for a man in order to go to bed with him.

Hastily he looked back out the window. He had no right to think these thoughts about her. How could he offer her love when he didn't even know his own name? Logic might dictate that his strong feelings for her stemmed from gratitude, but on a deep, elemental level, he knew that was pure bunk. He was falling in love with Maya because of the woman she was.

"Have you looked at these inserts of San Antonio and Houston?" she asked.

"A dozen times. Houston seemed more familiar at first, but now I can't be sure. It's hard to tell from a map."

"We could drive over there."

"To Houston? It's at least six hours away."

"San Antonio isn't that far. We could be there in an hour and a half." She closed the atlas and added, "I could make an appointment with a psychologist while we're there. One who's experienced in dealing with amnesia. A specialist might have some idea how to help you."

"Maybe that's a good idea."

"I'll get a reference from Uncle Garth and call this afternoon. In the meantime, I need to check on the new barn I'm having built. Would you like to ride over there with me?"

"Sure. Sounds good."

They went down to the barn behind the house, and Maya asked the hired hand there to saddle two horses.

"You speak very fluent Spanish," Adam observed.

"My mother taught me. I really don't know which was my first language. Do you have a feel for any other language?"

"None. I know a few Spanish phrases, of course. Most Texans do. I have no feel for German, so I guess I'm not from around New Braunfels."

The man led out two horses, and Maya swung lithely up onto the buckskin. Adam easily mounted the bay and automatically held the reins in his left hand.

"You know how to ride," she observed.

"It seems I do."

"Good. That comes in handy out here."

They nudged their mounts into an easy trot that was good for covering ground but not tiring to the horses. At first all the scenery looked pretty much alike to Adam, but as they rode, he began to notice the differences. Subtle shades of green, purple and gold colored the endless hills. Vistas appeared as they topped a ridge, only to vanish as they rode down the sloping shale. Prickly-pear cacti were everywhere, from the hills to the rock ledges. The mesquite and wiry oaks offered shade to rabbits and an occasional deer. Land that had seemed barren was in reality teeming with life, once he looked closely.

"Why are you building a barn way out here?" he asked.

"To store hay for winter feeding. Javier has to haul it out to the cows, and this will make his job easier. Some of the men are grading a road over there, but this way is a little shorter." She let her horse pick its way down a sharp incline, and Adam's followed, more sure-footed than any animal accustomed to flatland would have been.

The sun was ever present, ever powerful. Already the horses' necks were dark with sweat, and Adam's shirt clung damply to his back. Overhead the sky was a brassy blue with only the smallest of clouds lingering near the horizon.

"Does it ever rain here?" he called to Maya.

"Not often enough. Every summer I wonder if the Ranata will just dry up and blow away. Then fall finally gets here, and the rains come. You wouldn't believe it on days like this, but we actually have snow in the winter. And in the spring these hills are solid flowers. Not only the cacti, but bluebonnets and Indian paintbrushes and wine cups. It's so beautiful, it makes you ache with pleasure."

Adam still rode slightly behind her and was treated to a tantalizing view of the rear of her tight jeans. Her hips swayed with the gait of her horse, and her rounded thighs hugged the animal's barrellike belly. He forced himself to look away.

"I gather you also raise horses. What kind?"

"Quarter horses. I've always loved them. The cattle were Dad's pride and joy; the horses are mine. Tomás Salazar is my head groom. He shows them all over the state."

They reached the new barn site, where they dismounted and tied the horses in the shade of a Pine oak.

Maya hailed her foreman, and Javier ambled over to them, his nut-brown face as friendly as ever. *"Buenos días, patrona, señor."*

"Hello, Javier." She spoke in English so Adam could understand. "How much work has been done this week?"

"Poco," he said glumly. "That new man, Luis, he is a troublemaker."

"Oh?"

"I also think he is a wetback. He says very little about where he comes from."

Maya shaded her eyes to look at the man Javier was speaking about. All her employees were supposed to have legal status, but some, she knew, probably had forged papers. Javier was fiercely proud of his American citizenship, however, and took a dim view of illegal aliens.

"That Luis, him and Enrique are always fussing. You know Enrique—he's mean as a yard dog. It don't take much to set him off."

"Enrique is a good worker, though. Maybe I should talk to them."

"Can't hurt, *patrona*. Might help."

Maya left Adam examining the structure of the two-story barn and went to speak with Enrique. In Spanish she asked about his wife and children before mentioning Luis.

"He is bad. Real bad. I think maybe he is outlaw." Enrique frowned at his enemy, who was watching them closely. "He has no people. Only that *gringo* he rode in with, Buddy. I think they are big trouble."

Buddy, who was also working nearby, heard his name and looked over at them. He glanced past the woman at Adam and did a double take, then snapped his head around toward Luis.

Maya nodded. "I'll talk to them. Try not to let them bother you." As she walked toward Luis, Maya noted that Buddy sidled nearer. Just as well, she supposed. This way she could confront them both at once. Behind her she heard Enrique also moving closer. That made her a little uneasy. The men who had been with her for a long time were very protective of her, and a hothead like Enrique might be provoked to fight by even the slightest of remarks against her.

"*Señor,* I must talk to you," she said to Luis. "I hear there has been trouble."

Luis glared at Enrique. "He tell you that? Man, he was lying. Ain't no trouble but what he's causing."

Enrique and Buddy stepped closer. Maya made a pacifying gesture. "No one is trying to cause trouble. I only want my barn built. Can't you work together for a bit longer?"

Buddy nudged his friend and said in English, "Let's split, man."

"What for, man? We got money coming to us. Maybe the *señorita* here would like to go out on the town with us. Hey?" He leered at Maya.

That was all Enrique needed. He exploded in a torrent of angry Spanish and reached out to shove Luis. Buddy grabbed at Enrique, and the furious Mexican leveled him with one blow. Luis jabbed at Enrique and caught him in the stomach. Enrique doubled over but charged like a bull. Maya cried out as she saw the flash of a knife in Luis's hand. Suddenly Enrique was on his knees, clutching at his bloodied sleeve.

Maya felt Adam push her aside to safety and half crouch to face the knife-wielding Mexican.

"Come on," Adam said softly to Luis as he made a beckoning motion with his fingers.

"Adam, be careful!" Maya exclaimed.

Recognition flickered over Luis's face, and his eyes darted from side to side. He knew now what Buddy had been trying to tell him.

"Come on," Adam repeated, his eyes never leaving Luis's.

Suddenly the Mexican charged and made a swipe with his knife, but Adam was no longer there. Adam grabbed Luis's wrist as he passed and twisted it, making him drop the knife. Using the man's own momentum, Adam tossed Luis onto his back. Buddy leaped at Adam, but again Adam was as elusive as smoke. With a grunt, Buddy landed on top of Luis.

Javier, who had come running as soon as he realized there was trouble, reached them and hauled the two onto their feet. "You're fired! Get the hell out of here!"

Both Buddy and Luis scrambled to their feet, and after casting a frightened look back at Adam, they hurriedly left.

Maya knelt beside Enrique to examine the gash on his arm. "It could have been worse. Javier, drive him to Dr. Kadlecek and have this sewn up." She raised her voice to the other men, "The rest of you get back to work."

As Javier helped Enrique into the Jeep, she turned to Adam. "You're full of surprises."

"It was automatic."

"Unless I'm mistaken, that was judo. Where do you suppose you learned that?"

"No, it was aikido, but I don't know why I know it."

Maya watched him as he mounted his horse. He had known exactly what to do and had dispatched the men easily. "Why do you suppose they tried to attack you?

I expected Luis to back down once Enrique was out of the fight."

Adam shook his head. Something was tugging at his mind. Something about the way Luis had used the word *man*. Causing Adam great irritation, the trace of memory dissolved. "I don't know. I guess they were just troublemakers, like Javier said. I doubt you'll see them again."

"I hope not. They've only been here a little over a week, but I never liked their attitude."

Following Maya's lead, Adam reined his horse around, and together they rode down a gentle slope not far from the barn. To Adam's surprise, he saw a wide stream flowing lazily beneath river willows. "There's water here!"

"Of course. How else could we raise cattle? It's all a matter of knowing where to look. The hills and rocks hide it until you're practically upon it."

Adam dismounted and let his horse wade out to drink. "I remember how thirsty I was that night when I got to your house. I could have walked right by this stream and not known it was here."

"It's possible." She rode her horse into the water and let it lower its head. "It widens into a swimming hole farther downstream. We'll go down there one day."

The dark green water flowed indolently in the shade, offering an oasis from the heat of the day. Tiny emerald-green flies buzzed over the water's surface, and a school of gray minnows circled curiously around the horses' legs. Adam looked about in amazement. "It's incredible."

When the horses had finished, Maya rode out of the water, and they tied the animals. Adam helped Maya climb up onto a boulder that jutted out over the water. For a while they sat in the green-gold shade and enjoyed the respite from the sun.

"I'm glad those two men didn't hurt you," Maya said. "I still can't quite believe what happened."

"Neither can I. You know, it's funny, but the way they kept looking at me, it was almost as if they knew me."

"What could you possibly have in common with people like that?"

"Nothing, I guess. But somehow... Well, it doesn't matter. If they knew me, they would have said something or called me by name instead of trying to knife me."

"True."

"I've gotten to the point of looking for signs of recognition everywhere, even in people who'd have no reason to know me."

"Maybe we could write aikido associations and see if they have any record of you."

"That should be a neat trick, since we don't know my name or where to start looking. I don't even know if there are such associations in the first place." He stared moodily down at the stream.

Maya picked a leaf and drew it over the curve of his ear. When he batted it away, she said, "Smile. There are worse fates than being stranded on the Ranata."

"You're right about that."

His eyes were the same hue as the water, and the scent of his warm body stirred her senses. He never smelled of cologne or after-shave, but rather of soap and clean skin. "You smell good."

He laughed. "In this heat, that's good to know. So do you." He leaned nearer to her neck to breathe in her fragrance. "Jasmine and honeysuckle. That's how you smell. To look at you, I would have expected something more exotic. Like Joy perfume."

She smiled. "I'm just a simple country girl at heart."

"Sure you are. About as simple as an Einstein equation." He leaned nearer still and let his cheek brush hers. He hadn't meant to touch her, but she drew him like a magnet.

Maya felt the contact all the way down to her toes. His skin felt so good against hers. Breathlessly she turned her face so that only a shadow separated their lips. Tilting her head, she kissed him almost shyly.

He moved his lips over hers and ran the tip of his tongue along them as if hungry for the taste of her. Her nerve endings exploded with pleasure as he sensuously explored her mouth, and Maya swayed closer to him. The tips of her breasts grazed his shirtfront, and she felt the sensation jolt both her and Adam.

He put his arms around her and pulled her to him in mounting passion. Then, drawing back, he gazed down at her with raw desire—and saw an answering passion in her eyes. He cupped her face in his palm and kissed her with all the longing in his soul.

Maya was shaken when he released her, but she didn't have to ask why he had. She knew as well as he did that they must stop at once or not stop at all. She dared not meet his eyes, certain her face must be stamped with longing for him. She didn't want to stop, didn't want to be reasonable. She wanted to give herself to him and enjoy all the pleasures his kiss had promised. Never had a man stirred her like this.

Just when she thought she couldn't stand the strained silence another moment, Adam stood and held out his hand to help her off the boulder. She let his warm fingers close over hers, using all her willpower not to throw her arms around him. Their eyes met, and she saw that he, too, was struggling with himself.

Without speaking, they mounted their horses and rode out into the sweltering heat. Maya felt a trickle of sweat run down between her breasts. After Adam's kiss her nerves were on fire, and the least sensation made her tremble with eagerness for his touch. She let her horse break into a canter and tried not to imagine Adam caressing her, loving her.

Lunchtime back at the *hacienda* passed in heavy silence, until Adam tossed his napkin to the table and said, "We've got to do something about this!"

She jumped. "About what?"

He smiled slightly, as if he knew exactly what she had been thinking and was amused at her pretense of nonchalance. "We have to find out about me. Especially after what happened at the stream."

"You mean the kiss?" she asked with studied innocence.

"You know exactly what I mean. What if I'm a criminal or something?"

"Joe Bob Walters didn't have an APB or whatever they call it on you."

"Forgive me, but I don't hold much stock in Joe Bob's detective abilities. I think we should go in and look through his files for ourselves. Maybe by now someone has discovered I'm missing." He frowned. "You'd think *someone* would notice I'm gone."

"I know I certainly would," she said softly.

"All right. That's it. Will you drive me into town?"

Maya drove with precision but as if she had never heard of a speed limit. In a remarkably short time, she stopped her white Mercedes in front of the county sheriff's office.

"I thought you said town was forty-five minutes away," he said as he got out of the car and drew a deep breath.

"That's how long it takes Javier and Uncle Garth. I drive a bit faster."

"A bit."

She laughed and slid out of the white glove-leather seat. Everyone teased her about her driving, but she'd never had an accident.

As she straightened and headed for the door to the sheriff's office, Adam drank in her appearance. She had changed from jeans to a soft cotton dress of lemon yellow and had twisted her hair into a Gibson-girl bun on the top of her head. Tendrils of hair waved on the nape of her neck, making the style softly romantic.

Joe Bob was in his small office with his deputy, Norman Lloyd. An oscillating fan stirred the heavy air and ruffled the papers littering the metal desk. "Afternoon, Maya, Mr. Russell," Norman said cheerfully.

"You know me?" Adam asked in surprise.

"Joe Bob told me about you. I figured you must be the one he meant."

"We want to know if there are any new missing-persons reports," Maya said to the sheriff. "If you're busy, maybe we could look through the files for you."

"I guess you could," Joe Bob said reluctantly. "They're public knowledge and all." He shoved back his swivel chair and rolled to the file cabinet. "This here is what you want.'' He handed a dog-eared manila folder to Maya and dug through another drawer. "Check these, too. They're the new Wanted lists. You don't never know.''

"Thanks,'' Adam said grimly as he took the second folder.

Norman gave Maya his chair, and Adam pulled a straight-backed wooden chair forward. Drawing a steadying breath, they started sorting through the papers.

"Nothing,'' Adam said at last. "Not one description is anything at all like me.''

"Nothing here, either,'' she agreed.

"While you're in, I think you ought to let me fingerprint you,'' Joe Bob said. "I can send that out and see if the boys in Austin have anything on you.''

"You mean the missing-persons file has a fingerprint section?'' Maya asked.

"He means the criminal file,'' Adam said testily.

"If you ain't done nothing, you ain't got nothing to hide,'' Joe Bob pointed out.

Norman stared at him. "You mean to tell me you really can't remember *nothing*?''

"I can't remember who I am or where I came from or why I was on the Ranata,'' Adam said patiently. "I can, however, remember how to brush my teeth and who the governor is.''

"If that don't beat all,'' Norman marveled. "My wife don't know who's governor half the time.''

"Joe Bob, I really don't see any reason to fingerprint Adam,'' Maya said.

"How about you?'' Joe Bob said as he leaned accusingly toward Adam. "You object?'' His attitude implied that any objection would be considered an admission of guilt.

"No. I don't object." Adam met the sheriff glare for glare.

"Norman, go get the polygraph equipment," Joe Bob said as he pulled out the ink pad and paper. "We might as well do it up right."

"A lie-detector test?" Maya gasped. "Joe Bob, really!"

"I have nothing to hide," Adam said. "Let's get it over with."

Joe Bob took Adam's prints and photograph, then began the polygraph test. After the test was finished and Adam had told the truth with every answer, Joe Bob sat back with a frown. "These things aren't always foolproof, you know. A real good liar can throw it off."

"Joe Bob!" Maya glared at the sheriff as if she'd like to shake him.

"He's right," Adam said. "But I didn't lie."

Joe Bob went on to say, "You recall when Gabe Andrews stole those chickens from Lou Ann Farmstett? He passed the lie-detector test slicker'n a whistle."

"We caught him frying chicken that same night," Norman explained. "Everybody knows Gabe never owned a chicken in his life and was too cheap to buy one. He confessed and asked us in to eat supper with him." Norman chuckled. "Gabe's a character if there ever was one."

"I can assure you I'm not a chicken thief, and I don't even know Lou Ann Farmstett," Adam said through his teeth.

"He sure don't talk like one, Joe Bob," Norman confirmed.

"Maybe not, but part of protecting the people of La Avenida is to be real careful of strangers. Mr. Russell, I think you really ought to consider moving to the motel. This is a small town, and folks talk."

"Oh?" Adam said with deceptive calm. "What do folks say?"

"They say it looks real funny, you staying out at the Ranata. Everybody knows Maya is a single lady living alone in that house. Up till now."

Adam leaned across the desk, forcing Joe Bob to pull back. In a carefully measured voice he said, "You pass the word to these 'folks' that if I ever hear even a whisper of scandal about Maya, they'll have to answer to me. You'll do that, won't you, Joe Bob?" His icy green eyes confirmed the threat that his words implied.

Joe Bob stared at him speechlessly.

Adam straightened and said to Maya, "Let's go. I'm sure the good sheriff will let us know if he hears anything."

As they went back out into the heat, Maya said, "You shouldn't antagonize Joe Bob. He means well."

"I don't care what he says about me, but when it comes to you, that's a different matter."

Maya smiled. She had never had anyone stand up for her before, and she decided she liked it. "How about spaghetti for supper? There's an Italian restaurant here that's really good."

Adam hesitated. "I don't like spending your money."

"Look, if the tables were reversed, you'd pay my way. Consider it a loan."

"I still don't like it."

"Okay. I'm going to eat spaghetti and garlic bread, and you can watch."

"Garlic bread?"

"With lots of gooey butter. *And* spumoni."

"I can't pass up spumoni. Let's go. But when I get myself back home, you can move in with me for however long I've stayed with you." He paused, afraid he had gone too far.

"I might just take you up on that," Maya said easily.

The restaurant was small and dark, with red-checkered plastic tablecloths, but Adam found she hadn't exaggerated about the quality of the food.

"You know," she said as she watched him finish off his dessert, "you don't quite fit in a place like this. Somehow you seem more the crystal-and-linen sort. The kind of person who knows what wine is saucy and which is delicate."

"That sounds disgustingly stuffy," he said with a laugh. "Do I really seem like that?"

"Not the stuffy part. Just sophisticated." She rested her chin on her palm and said, "Maybe you're a prince traveling incognito."

"I wouldn't be a bit surprised. When Dr. Kadlecek sewed me up, was the blood red or blue?"

"Darn. That blows that theory."

"Maybe I'm a Gypsy."

"With blond hair? I doubt it."

"You know what I hope? I hope we find out I'm just an ordinary person with ordinary dreams and no encumbrances."

"Somehow I can't picture you as ordinary at all."

Adam covered her fingers with his and gently rubbed his thumb over the back of her hand. After a long time he said, "Where are we going, Maya? Are you just playing a game with me?"

She met his eyes and said quietly, "I never play games."

Chapter Five

Adam sat impatiently while the doctor removed the stitches from his forehead. Garth was in no hurry and couldn't be rushed. "Looks like it healed just fine," he said as he pushed his glasses farther up on his nose. "There won't be much of a scar at all. Your hair will cover it."

"But I still don't remember anything. Isn't there something to make my memory come back?"

"Nope. Nothing but time."

Adam stood and paced to the window and back. "Are you sure a person always gets his memory back?"

"I've been doing some reading on it, and I'm sorry to say this, but amnesia has been permanent in some cases. I didn't want to tell you because I saw no reason to worry you unnecessarily, but it could happen. I really expected you to be improving by now."

"You mean I may never find out who I am?"

"Could be. On the other hand, you might start remembering at any time."

"Damn." Adam ran his fingers through his hair in frustration. "I've got a life out there somewhere. Surely *somebody* is missing me by now. Even if I don't have a family, I must have a job or friends or...or something!"

"Maybe, maybe not."

"I don't feel like a loner, a drifter."

The doctor shrugged.

Looking over at him, Adam said, "You have something against me. What is it?"

"I don't have a thing in this world against you personally. I'm just thinking about Maya. I've always been like a second father to her. Not only was her father my partner, he was my best friend too. I don't want to see her get hurt."

"Neither do I."

"I know it's none of my business, but she's starting to care for you. Even I can see that. But what can you offer her? You don't even know if you're married or single," he said bluntly.

"I *feel* single," Adam argued.

"That's not the same thing. At your age most men are married."

"Or divorced."

"Maybe."

"Dr. Kadlecek, I care for her, too. Don't you think I've been over all this time and again in my mind?"

The older man nodded. "Like I said, I'm thinking about Maya. I just don't want her to get hurt."

"If I never get my memory back, I'll always be just what I am now," he said thoughtfully. "No roots, no ties."

"On the other hand, does that make you free to start all over and mix in other people's lives, just because you don't remember your commitments?"

"What do you suggest? Should I lock myself away and not get close to anyone on the off chance that I may have someone or something to keep me away from her?"

Dr. Kadlecek gave Adam an appraising look. "I'm just saying don't leap into anything with Maya that could be awkward later on. She's the kind of person who doesn't get over hurt very easily."

Adam wanted to argue or at least tell the doctor to mind his own business, but he knew the man was thinking of Maya. "I'm the last person on earth who would hurt her."

The doctor nodded as if he hoped Adam was right. "Well, physically, you're perfectly well. I guess I'd better go look in on Rosa Salazar and the baby. Be seeing you around."

Adam looked thoughtfully after the doctor. Soon he would have to make some decisions. Above all, he would have to be very careful not to let himself fall more deeply in love with Maya.

He did love her, he knew. No matter what else he tried to call it, he could recognize love. He didn't know if she loved him, and he was afraid to find out. If she didn't, he would be hurt to the core. If she did, he couldn't make a commitment to her—and he wanted very much to do just that.

He went out to the horse barn in search of her. The building was open at both ends to let a breeze through, but even the wind was hot and oppressive. The warm scents of hay and feed, horses and leather, permeated the area.

Maya was still in a stall near the end, currying a shiny black horse. When she heard Adam approach, she looked up and smiled. He leaned on the wooden gate and watched as she brushed the large animal. She wore tight jeans and a faded pink shirt tied at her waist. Her hair was plaited into a single braid that was as thick as her wrist and hung to her waist.

"Did you get the stitches out?" she asked.

"All done," he confirmed. "Maya, I've been thinking. Maybe Joe Bob is right, and I should move to town."

She looked at him in surprise.

"I could get a job doing something. I can't keep living off your hospitality."

"I don't see why not. The Ranata would be in pretty bad shape if it couldn't support a houseguest for a few weeks."

"It may not be just a few weeks. What if my amnesia is permanent? It may be, you know."

"I know. I read Dad's medical books." She quit brushing the horse and studied him. "Do you want to leave?"

"No." When she looked at him with her eyes large and troubled, he couldn't bear the idea of leaving her. "I don't want to go. It's something I feel I should do."

"I have a rule," she said as she gave the horse a farewell pat. "I never do the things I *should* or *ought*. So far, it's carried me quite well through life. If you don't want to leave, then don't."

He opened the gate for her, then fastened it behind her. "And what sort of man will I be if I don't?"

"Actually, I was hoping you might help me out with my bookkeeping. I can do it, but it's a chore I detest. I'll trade you a job for your room and board."

He looked unconvinced, so she added, "Really, Adam, you shouldn't go unless you want to leave."

"Bookkeeping, huh?"

"Don't look at me that way. I really *don't* like to do it. You can ask Uncle Garth."

"I will. I don't want charity."

"I'll work you to exhaustion. I also need someone to help out in the stables occasionally. Tomás is getting some horses ready for a show, and one of the grooms quit unexpectedly."

He decided to trust her sincere bid for his help. "All right. You talked me into it."

She looked past him to the late-model powder-blue Buick pulling around the house.

"Company?" he asked.

"That's Shelley Cooper's car. She's buying that black horse I was grooming. Come and meet her. She and her husband, Ed, are our nearest neighbors."

He noticed her unconscious use of the word *our* and felt much too pleased over it. This, he tried to tell himself, was no way to maintain his emotional distance.

A slender blonde with very tanned skin got out of the car and came to meet them at the barn door. "Maya, I've come to bring you a check for Lady's Choice." She stared frankly at Adam as she spoke. "I didn't know you had company."

"I don't. Shelley, this is Adam Russell. Adam, Shelley Cooper."

"You...aren't company?" Shelley asked in confusion. "I didn't know Maya and anyone...that is..."

She thrust a covered bowl into Maya's hands. "I brought you some *gazpacho*."

"Thank you." To Adam, Maya said, "Shelley makes the best *gazpacho* in the county."

He grinned and took the cold bowl from Maya. "I'll take it in to Lupe."

Shelley stared after him until he was out of earshot before saying, "Who is he?"

"Would you believe I found him on my doorstep?"

"Not in a million years."

"It's true. He showed up one night nearly two weeks ago, all bruised and bloody. Uncle Garth fixed him up, but he has amnesia."

"You're kidding! Nobody gets amnesia! Not really." She thought for a minute. "Wait a minute, is this the man you called us about? The one who said he'd worked for us?"

"Yes. He was trying to keep us from learning he couldn't remember. It's a fairly common response to the trauma of amnesia. He can't remember his name or anything about his past."

Shelley stared at her. "He isn't living here! In your house? Just the two of you?"

"Don't have a fit, Shelley, it's nothing immoral. He's staying in the guest room."

"Well, I should hope so! You can't let a strange man just move into your house!"

"Adam isn't all that strange."

"You know what I mean. Why, he could be a...a...anything! How do you know he won't steal you blind or murder you in your sleep or something?"

"You sound just like Joe Bob Walters. Adam is perfectly trustworthy. In fact," she added softly, "he's pretty special."

"Surely you aren't . . ."

"No, we aren't," Maya said testily.

"I didn't mean to offend you. It's just that his being here took me by surprise."

"You must not have been to town lately. According to Joe Bob, Adam is the hottest gossip going."

"I can see why." Shelley looked toward the door through which Adam had disappeared. "Nobody that good-looking ever passed out on my front porch."

Maya heard the envy in her friend's voice and exclaimed, "That's a fine way to talk! What about Ed?"

"I adore Ed, but he sure doesn't look like this Adam of yours."

"He's not *my* Adam. Incidentally, he's working as my bookkeeper and helping out in the stable."

"He could keep books for me any day."

"Shelley!"

"Well, I may be married, but I'm not blind."

"Come see your horse," Maya said to divert her.

They walked back into the barn, and Shelley asked, "What do you really know about him?"

"Lady's Choice? He's a gelding by Gambler's Luck out of Lady Be Good. When I have his papers switched over to you, you can read the rest."

"Not the horse—Adam."

"I told you, he has amnesia."

"But he looks perfectly healthy."

"He is. He simply has no memory."

"Maya, I really think you're taking a chance. I mean, people like us can't take just anyone into our homes."

"Like us?" Maya asked innocently.

"You know what I mean. When you have money, you have to be more careful."

Maya had always taken her wealth more or less for granted, but she was reminded that the Coopers' fortune had come fairly recently from oil wells. "I'm not afraid."

"You should be! I can't believe Dr. Kadlecek is letting you do this."

"Uncle Garth could hardly stop me," Maya said with a laugh.

"Don't you remember those rapes over in Kerrville last month? They never have caught the man, and Kerrville isn't all that far away."

"Adam is no rapist! Shelley, he's been living here almost two weeks and has never made any threatening moves at all."

"Then there were the serial murders in Uvalde."

"Uvalde is a long way from here, and they caught the killer."

"Nevertheless, it just shows that such things happen. What if he's hiding out from the law and is merely pretending to have amnesia?"

"Impossible. He let Joe Bob fingerprint him and send his picture all over the state and goodness knows where else. No one has ever heard of him."

"That may not be a good sign. They say the most difficult criminals to catch are the ones who have no records."

"If he was hiding out from the law, he'd hardly have agreed to let Joe Bob take his prints and photo or do a polygraph test."

"Joe Bob did that, too? Does he suspect him of something?"

"Are you kidding? Joe Bob would arrest his own shadow for jaywalking!"

Shelley looked unconvinced. "Just the same, be careful."

"I will be. Okay?" She opened the stall and led the black horse out, wondering if she was too trusting or if everyone else was too suspicious.

That night Lupe served dinner on the back patio. The only illumination was from the slender candles in terra-cotta holders and the strings of tiny Christmas lights draped over the rough wood ceiling. The table was old, its wide planks weathered to a silvery color. The utensils had handles made from antlers worn smooth from years of use, and the glasses were hand-blown crystal that shaded from blue to amber.

"You've been very quiet since your friend left," Adam remarked as he sipped his margarita. "Did she say something that upset you?"

"No, no," Maya replied a bit too quickly. "It's just that I get moody when I sell one of the horses, and Lady's Choice was a favorite of mine."

"Then why did you sell him?"

"I can't keep them all. Besides, they all tend to be favorites with me one way or another."

"If I were a friend of yours," he said casually as he rolled the flour *tortilla* around the *fajita*'s ingredients, then tucked the end over, "and I found a strange man living here, I'd give you all kinds of warnings."

Maya glanced at him as she spooned a *chilies rellenos* onto her plate. She found it unnerving that he often seemed to read her mind.

"I'd ask tons of questions and probably scare the wits out of you—all for your own good."

"She did mention a few things along that line."

"I thought she might have. Maya, I can't say I've never done anything wrong, but I can promise you have nothing to fear from me."

"I know that."

"Then why is your fork shaking?"

She laid down her fork and looked out at the night. "I guess it's the heat. It's been so long since we had any rain."

"Are you being honest with me?"

"More or less."

Adam smiled, and she felt her heart lurch. When he looked at her that way, she couldn't possibly believe ill of him.

"Maybe you should keep a gun in the house," he teased.

"I do."

"You do?"

"Of course. But I rarely take potshots at guests."

"You constantly amaze me. I would have sworn you wouldn't touch a gun with a stick."

"Around here kids learn to ride and shoot as a part of growing up. I only target shoot, though. It's against my principles to kill things."

"But you eat meat," he said good-naturedly as he gestured at the *fajita*.

Her teeth flashed in the candlelight. "As you've mentioned before, I'm a mass of contradictions."

Beyond the darkened yard a coyote howled, sending a mournful message over the hills. The cry was quickly picked up and passed on by another.

Adam looked out at the darkness. "It sounds like a dozen of them, but there are really only a couple. They have a remarkable range of notes."

"I know. But I'm surprised that you do. Maybe you *are* from around here."

"Coyotes are everywhere in the state. All it means is that I haven't lived in a city my whole life. Or at least that I occasionally make trips into the country."

An armadillo, attracted to the lights, ambled almost onto the porch, stopped at a movement Maya made, then wandered back into the shadows.

"Strange little animals," Adam commented. "They look like miniature armored tanks."

"Shelley was quite captivated by you, in between her dire warnings. You're lucky you stumbled onto the Ranata instead of the Lazy C."

"Where I'll be safe?" he finished for her.

Maya avoided his eyes. She wasn't sure she was any more to be trusted in that area than her neighbor. "She's mainly all talk. She and Ed are quite solidly married."

"That's good to know," he replied.

She glanced at him and found he was teasing her. "More *guacamole*?"

"No, thanks. A little avocado goes a long way with me. But it was good."

For dessert Lupe had made flan, and Maya savored the cool, caramel-flavored custard. Even though the sun had gone down, the heat was still oppressive. Far away in the black sky, silent lightning flared, exposing the tops of towering clouds.

"There's the rain you wanted," Adam remarked.

"No way. That's just heat lightning. We won't see a drop." Again the sky glared pale yellow. "At least it makes a pretty display."

Lupe cleared away the dishes, but they stayed seated at the table. The leather and wicker basket chairs were comfortable, and there was the occasional bonus of a breeze or two.

"I really should install central air-conditioning," Maya commented. "Every summer I threaten to do it, but then I look at the *hacienda* and think how the ducting would alter the ceilings, so I put it off another year. This summer has been unusually hot."

"There's a way to duct so the pipes won't show and you wouldn't have to lower the ceilings."

"Oh?"

"I vaguely recall seeing an old Victorian house that was cooled without ruining the lines."

"Maybe it was your own house."

"I don't think so. I don't have a strong feeling for it." As he spoke, however, a memory did flash through his mind. He was riding on a motorcycle, and the day was blisteringly hot. As fast as the image had come, it vanished. Carefully he put down his margarita and tried to pull back the thought. "A motorcycle," he said slowly. "I remember a motorcycle. And the heat. And a road that seemed to stretch forever."

"A motorcycle?" she asked, leaning forward.

He shook his head. "It's gone again. All I recall is that one or two seconds."

"It's a beginning! You're going to get it all back!" She was glad for his sake, but she was also slightly upset. When his memory returned, Adam would leave.

The ghostly lightning traced an arc of fire from one cloud to another. Adam gazed at the display in wonder. "All that lightning and no thunder at all."

Maya stood and walked to one of the thick, rough-hewn columns that supported the roof. "Aren't you excited over remembering something?"

"Yes. No. I don't know what to feel. The memory is so short, and I have no idea if it's recent or from my boyhood. I'm almost afraid to get my hopes up. What if that one flash is all there ever is?"

"At least you know you had a motorcycle at one time or another."

"Just like thousands of other people. It still doesn't tell me who I am." He got up and joined her, leaning on the other side of the post. "If I get too excited, maybe I'll jinx having more memories."

"I don't think it works that way."

He peered around the column to view her face in the dim light. "In some ways I don't want to remember anything beyond the Ranata." He looked back at the flashing sky. "Can you understand that?"

"Yes," she answered softly. "I understand perfectly."

He circled the post, and she found herself half enclosed in his arms as he gazed down at her. "You remind me of the stormy sky. There's more going on than meets the ear." He stroked her cheek and ran his fingers through her loose hair to cup the back of her head. "What thoughts are running around in there? What are you feeling and hoping?"

Maya moistened her parted lips at the implied intimacy of his words. Slowly she shook her head. There were things she dared not say to him.

"A woman of mystery, my Maya. A woman of contradictions." He ran his fingers through her thick hair, gathered it like a silken skein, then caressed her cheek and neck with it. "Even your name is exotic. You weave the spell of a Lorelei, then pull back within yourself and leave me wondering."

Silent and as full of tumult as the stormy sky, she gazed up at him. Slowly he bent and hesitated just over her parted lips before covering them with his own. He pulled her to him until her body molded perfectly with his and her breasts flattened against his chest.

Maya met his searching tongue with her own and tasted the trace of salt on his lips from the margarita. Sensuously she returned his kiss as fireworks seemed to explode within her. The hot breeze eddied about them, stoking their passion rather than cooling their skin. She felt his hot palms caress the contours of her back and hips through the thin cotton of her peasant blouse and gathered skirt.

He murmured her name into the curve of her neck as she let her hands memorize the hard swells of his back muscles and the indentation of his spine. He wore a pale blue knit pullover, and when her hands slipped beneath it to touch his skin, she trembled as if the contact seared her. His flesh was firm and warm and the texture of fine satin. Beneath his fingers she felt his strength, leashed but certain. Adam was a powerful man, and she felt delicate in his embrace.

Again he kissed her, and Maya felt as if the world and all its restraints were dissolving. She had never known anyone who could kiss this way. He was masterful, like a man in love.

His hands explored her ribs, and his thumb traced the lower swell of her breast. All her senses reeled as she willed him to touch her, to release the emotions she had held back for so long. Her nipples and loins ached with wanting him to touch her, to taste her flesh, to take her into the coolness of the house and make love to her throughout the sultry night.

With tantalizing slowness, as if he had all eternity to savor her, Adam ran his fingers up her arm and over her chest, following the low neckline of the peasant blouse. Maya could scarcely contain herself as he kissed her into submission and his long fingers slowly, ever so slowly, untied the ribbon that gathered the blouse.

The blouse yielded to his touch and slid off her shoulders to reveal her naked breasts. Maya murmured as he almost reverently stroked the firm globes and cupped them gently in his hands. He rolled one nipple between his thumb and forefinger, and she felt as if she would explode like the roiling clouds above. The faint wind teased her bare skin, and she wanted to strip away their clothes and love him until the fire inside her was no longer a torment.

She swayed as his kisses made her weak inside, and her nipple beaded eagerly against his palm. His knowing fingers strummed her to aching desire, and she wondered how she could bear the delicious agony.

"Maya," he whispered into the night cloud of her hair. "My Maya."

"Adam," she murmured with all the longing of her soul. "Adam, love me."

He grew still under her hands, and she wondered frantically what she had said to make him stop. "Adam?" she whispered uncertainly.

"That's just it," he said in a pained voice. "I'm not Adam. I'm not anybody."

"Is that what's wrong?" she asked in confusion.

"Isn't that enough?" he said roughly as he released her and turned away to glare out at the night.

Maya slowly pulled her blouse back up to cover her nakedness. She felt torn and abandoned but was far too proud to let him know.

"You asked me to love you," he ground out as he turned back to face her. "How can I love you when I don't even know who I am?" Although he frowned at her, she could see the raw pain in his eyes. "I'm sorry, Maya. I won't let it happen again." Abruptly he stalked back into the house.

Maya stared after him, not knowing what to think or where to turn. She had let down her barriers, and he had gotten closer to her than she had allowed any man to be in a very long time, and then he'd backed away. Embarrassment flooded over her, and she wasn't sure if she was more hurt or more angry.

Quickly she let herself into her bedroom and locked the door. Her breath was still coming in ragged gasps. What had she been thinking of to let him practically take her right there on the patio? She could still feel the touch of his hands and lips and the way their bodies had responded to each other. Her skin still burned with longing for him, and she was terribly afraid she would rush back to him if he knocked on her door.

She ran to her bathroom and flooded the room with light. Gripping the countertop, she stared at her pale face in the large mirror. Her eyes were enormous and so dark they were almost black. Her hair was disheveled and her lips slightly swollen from the passion of their kisses. The image in the mirror didn't look at all like Maya Kingsley, *patrona* of the Ranata.

Hastily Maya shucked off her clothes and turned on the cold-water tap of the shower, then stepped in and let the cool jets of water pound against her hot skin until she had regained some of her composure.

As the water sluiced over her, she made fervent promises that she knew she couldn't keep, for if he kissed her again in the hot night, she knew she would react in exactly the same way. She finally turned off the shower. She could cool her body but not her mind.

Across the dark house, Adam stood in his own shower, his head under the stream of cold water. He still could scarcely believe he had let himself get so far out of control. Hell, he had practically taken her right there on the table. She had trusted him, taken him into her home, even saved his life, and he had treated her as if he were a normal man with a background and a name! True, she had returned his kisses, and he had found more passion in her than he had expected. But that wasn't the point. He had no right to her kisses or to hear her murmur his name under the flickering night sky. His name—if only he knew that much!

The memory of her soft but firm breasts in his hands and her fingers beneath his shirt made him groan. He wanted her so badly he ached, cold shower or no cold shower. He cursed himself for ever having let things go so far. She would be entirely within her rights to demand that he leave the next day. For a while he tortured himself with the idea of never seeing Maya again, but the thought was too painful.

Somehow, he vowed, somehow he would keep his emotions under control. He closed his eyes and let the cold water flow over him.

Chapter Six

I called Joe Bob this morning, and there's still no missing-persons report on you," Maya said as they sat on a tree trunk growing parallel to the ground, overlooking the river.

Adam frowned as he twirled a willow leaf between his fingers. "How can someone disappear and no one care enough to report it?"

"That's a bigger mystery than where you came from, if you ask me."

They had been polite but cautious with each other all day, the near-seduction of the night before still playing through their minds.

"You must have come from some other part of the country. Someone may be tearing up Ohio or South Dakota looking for you."

He shook his head. "I have no feel for any state but Texas. It's too familiar to me."

"So was Colorado."

"Not as much."

She leaned back against a limb and wondered why Adam was being so distant. To observe him, one would think *he* was the one who'd made a fool of himself, rather than she. She watched him toss a pebble into the water, then pulled a notepad and pen from her pocket. "Let's try word association. I'll say a word, and you give me a one-word response. Maybe it will trigger some memories."

"Why not?" he said grimly.

She flipped to an empty page and poised her pen as she thought. "Work?"

"Daily."

"That's good. You must have had a steady job."

He gave her a level look.

"Job?"

"Inside."

"Salary?"

"Good."

"Home?"

"Town."

"State?"

"Texas."

"City?"

"State."

She nibbled on the end of her pen. This wasn't as productive as she had hoped. Then, with sudden inspiration, she said, "Man."

"Woman."

"Woman?"

"Wife."

"Name?"

"Address."

"Wife?"

"Love."

"Love?"

He hesitated. He had almost said "Maya." Instead he substituted, "Forever."

"You're supposed to give your first thought. You paused."

He shrugged.

Maya put away the pen and pad and leaned her forearms on her jeans-clad knees. "I thought that would be too simple."

"I guess all we can do is wait."

The leaves of the willow and cottonwood trees above them drooped in the heat and harsh sunlight. In the yellowing grasses insects begged for rain. Adam wiped beads of sweat from his brow and looked longingly at the water. "I thought it would be cooler here."

"I had hoped so, too." She turned back to the horses and said, "I guess we should ride back."

"Maya, wait," he said as she started to rise. He caught her wrist and gently pulled her back down on the misshapen tree trunk. "I'm sorry about last night."

For a moment she was silent as she wondered if he meant he was sorry it had happened or sorry because her kisses hadn't pleased him. "That's all right."

"It won't happen again."

"Okay."

"Just like that? 'Okay'?"

"I can see how something like...that...could come between us. After all, we're sharing the same house. It's not as if we're dating and can simply not go out with each other if we regret becoming too intimate."

"I'm not into one-night stands," he said almost angrily.

"No? How do you know?"

"It sounds as if you are, however. Are you accustomed to making love with a man and then not seeing him again?"

"No!"

"Then why did you say such a thing?"

The volume of her voice rose to meet his. "I was giving you an out, since you so obviously regret having kissed me last night. After all, *I'm* not the one who tried to seduce *you*."

"No? That's not the way I remember it!"

"What?" She leaped to her feet and stood glaring at him. He rose to tower over her. "Who kissed who first?"

"What difference does it make, since it won't ever happen again?"

"No? What do you think about this!" She grabbed his head and yanked him down to plant a kiss on his lips, then pushed him away. "Don't you tell *me* who I will or won't kiss!"

"Don't push your luck with me, Maya!"

"No? What will you do?"

He yanked her to him and kissed her hard, masterfully.

"You!" she sputtered in rage. "How dare you kiss me back! Of all the gall!" She backed away from him, her fists clenched at her side.

"I wouldn't keep backing up if I were you," he warned.

"No? This is *my* world, Adam Russell—or whoever you are! I do as I please!"

"Suit yourself." He folded his arms over his chest and gave her a maddening smile.

Just to prove her point, Maya took another step backward. The heel of her boot found only air, and for a moment she teetered on the bank, then fell backward into the river. She came up soaked and furious.

"I told you not to back up," he said mildly.

"Help! I can't reach bottom here!"

With sudden concern, Adam hurried nearer the bank and reached out to catch her hand. Her slippery fingers slid away, but then he caught her. Before he knew what she was doing, Maya pulled hard. With a surprised shout he tumbled into the water and came up sputtering.

"I'd say we're about even now," Maya said smugly. When she saw the look in his eyes, she quickly began to edge toward the bank. "Uh-oh. Adam, don't look at me like that."

He shook his hair out of his eyes and waded purposefully toward her. Maya tried to scramble up the bank, but she couldn't find a handhold on the slick mud and grass. Before she could clear the water, he grabbed the waistband of her jeans and hauled her back into the water.

"Now I'd say we're even. You fell in the first time on your own."

Maya swung at him, but the muddy ground beneath her feet gave way, throwing her against him. Before she could pull away, he caught her tightly.

"Quit struggling or I'll duck you again," he threatened.

"You do and I'll drown you!"

To her surprise, he laughed. "You're some hellcat, aren't you? It's a shame you didn't have brothers to take you down a peg or two."

"*If* they could," she retorted.

With a laugh he hauled her up to his level and kissed her. At first she resisted, but she wasn't as iron-willed as she had planned to be. Before she knew it, she was kissing him back.

"You taste like river water," he said as he let her slide down his lean body. "Cool and a little fishy," he teased.

"So do you," she retorted, though she really couldn't work up a convincing case of indignation.

Again he bent and kissed her. His tongue tasted the warm moistness of her mouth, and Maya molded her body to his to savor every inch of him.

"So much for our good intentions," he said huskily as he lifted his head.

"We'll just have to try harder." She found it difficult to breathe when he was gazing at her like that. His eyes were the same color as the dark leaves overhead, and his hair was plastered into a cap of pure gold.

"Yes," he said at last as he reached up to brush the beads of river water off her eyelashes. "We'll try harder."

She stared up at him, not wanting him to remove his arm from around her or to step away. "Otherwise things could get out of hand. I guess."

His riveting gaze held her, and she found herself memorizing the straight line of his nose, the Germanic strength of his jaw, the way his lips looked sweet and sensuous all at the same time.

"I suppose we ought to get out of the river," she said at last, though she didn't make a move to do so.

"Yes. I suppose we should. Maya, do you want me to leave?" he asked unexpectedly.

Her lips parted, and her startled eyes met his. "No," she said at last.

He smiled, and she felt her knees turn to jelly. "No, don't leave," she said.

Adam kept his arm around her as he helped her wade toward the bank. He put both his hands on her slender waist and half lifted her up the muddy slope. Maya reached back to help pull him out.

For a moment they studied each other as if they weren't so sure what to make of themselves. Then they walked to their horses, their boots squishing with every step.

Maya led Lady's Choice out of the stall and down the central aisle, the horse walking daintily, as if his hooves were made of glass. The heat of the day had swollen the veins in his gracefully arched neck, and when Maya led him out into the sunshine, his black coat gleamed like patent leather.

Adam had backed the pickup and horse trailer around to the front of the barn and was swinging open the tailgate. Like all the farm equipment on the Ranata, it was painted sky blue.

The horse snorted, pranced sideways and tossed his long mane sideways when he saw the trailer. Maya spoke to him in the gentling tone she used to calm her animals, using the language of her childhood—a combination of English, Spanish and sibilant sounds of her own devising. The horse quieted but continued to eye the metal contraption uneasily.

"He's afraid of trailers," Maya explained. "He always has been, for some reason."

Adam patted the horse's sleek neck and rubbed its ears beneath the red webbed halter. Yet when he tried to lead the animal in, the horse balked and tossed his head defiantly. At Maya's suggestion, Adam walked him in a circle that brought him back to the gate opening, but Lady's Choice stopped short of entering and snorted again.

Maya got a handful of feed and tried to bribe the horse into the trailer, but still he balked.

"Maybe we should put a rope behind him and scoot him in," Adam suggested.

"No, he might get a rope burn." Again she tried tricking the animal by leading him in a circle that ended at the trailer's gate, but the horse pawed the ground, and when she pulled on the lead rope, he backed up stubbornly.

Adam went around behind and waved his hands and whistled, but Lady's Choice pranced in a tight arc and refused to budge. Again Maya hauled on the lead rope, even jumping into the trailer herself to encourage him. The horse reared slightly and rolled his eyes.

"I could ride him over to the Coopers'," Adam suggested. "You could meet me there and bring me home."

"The Lazy C is miles away. Besides, it's too hot. Look at him; he's already starting to sweat." She got a cloth and wiped the gelding's shiny body. "I can't deliver a horse that's lathered like a mad dog. Of all the days for Tomás to be off!" She sat down on the trailer floor and frowned at the horse.

Adam joined her. "Why is he so afraid of trailers?"

"I don't know," she said with disgust to show the horse how displeased she was. "His mama is that way about bridges. She wouldn't cross a wooden bridge if her life depended on it. I think it has to do with the sound their hooves make. I have another horse that won't cross running streams, and another one that goes crazy if he sees something flutter. Who can figure out horses' brains?''

"I don't guess you could call Shelley and tell her you'll deliver Lady's Choice tomorrow when Tomás is back?"

"What reason could I give her? That I can't put a horse into a trailer? I can't call Tomás; he and Rosa have gone to Presidio to show the new baby to her parents."

Lady's Choice reached out and daintily nibbled the bottom of Maya's loose cotton shirt. She pushed the black velvet nose away. "Don't try to make up with me. You're causing me a lot of grief."

Adam leaned his elbow on one of the hot side rails and asked, "Well? What do we do now? I could go find one of your workers and see if he can help. If we join hands behind the horse and hold on to the trailer, we may be able to shove him in."

"And get your brains kicked out at the same time. Your memory is already bad enough. Kicking is another of his bad habits." Suddenly her frown faded, and she grinned. "Wait a minute! I know what we can do." She gave Adam the horse's lead and hurried back into the barn.

Minutes later she came out carrying a soft cotton rope about a yard long. Adam looked concerned. "You aren't going to hit him, are you?"

"Of course not. You get ready to shut the back gate once he's in." She looped the rope around one of the horse's front feet just below the fetlock. Lady's

Choice lifted his roped foot to paw, and she pulled the foot easily forward onto the bed of the trailer. At the same time she tugged on the lead rope, causing the horse to shift his weight forward. Repeating the action, Maya encouraged another step, and soon his momentum had brought him fully into the trailer. Adam quickly closed the gate to block his escape.

Maya tied the horse's head to the front end so he couldn't move about and patted the animal triumphantly. "It worked! I saw that done once when a rodeo was moving out, but I've never tried it before." She climbed over the top and down to stand beside Adam. "I'll have to remember that!"

She drove along the narrow farm-to-market route, her elbow resting on the open window. "All of this is the Ranata," she said over the gusts of hot wind, gesturing well beyond the road.

"How many acres do you have?" he shouted back.

Maya's even white teeth flashed in a laugh. "There are two questions you never ask a rancher: how many acres you have, and how many head of cattle?"

Adam laughed and shook his head. He had learned to love this woman and her untamed land so quickly! Yet it somehow seemed he had always loved her.

To Adam the Lazy C property was indistinguishable from that of the Ranata, but the ranch house was quite different. Built of red brick, the Coopers' home contrasted sharply with the baked yellow ground, and the small yard around it had been coaxed into a flower garden that looked like something that belonged in suburbia.

"They haven't been here long," Maya said almost in apology. "Only fifteen years."

Adam was still digesting this when she pulled to a stop and jumped down to let the horse out of the trailer. Lady's Choice was much easier to unload as he backed hastily onto the gravel drive.

The front door opened, and Shelley, clad in white shorts and a skimpy halter top, called over her shoulder to Ed. She hurried across the yard to the horse. "He's gorgeous!" she gushed.

"He's all yours." Maya handed her the lead rope and gave Lady's Choice a final pat.

"Ed, hurry. Come see," Shelley called toward the house.

A man of medium build, with thinning hair, stepped out onto the narrow porch. "Well! So here he is," he said with a grin. "We could have come after him."

"No," said Maya. "Delivery was part of our deal. Besides," she said with an amused glance at Adam, "he was no trouble."

"None to speak of," Adam agreed. He held out his hand to the man. "I'm Adam Russell. I met your wife yesterday."

"Ed Cooper," the man said as he sized up the stranger. "Yes, Shelley mentioned you."

Maya raised her eyebrows at her friend as Shelley hastily changed the subject. "Isn't Lady's Choice a beauty? I've never seen such an animal."

"Pity he's a gelding," Ed agreed.

"Otherwise he wouldn't be reliable to ride," Maya explained. "Besides, his chest is a bit narrow for breeding stock, and his rump is off somewhat."

"I don't care. I think he's a love." Shelley smoothed a hand over the satiny hide. "I'll treat him like royalty."

"I know you will. I hope when I die I come back as one of your horses," Maya teased. "I can't imagine an easier life." To Adam she said, "Ed even has soft music piped into the stable and burlap covering the stalls' walls."

Ed grinned at her as if he were accustomed to her teasing and enjoyed it. "I read once that all that pleases horses."

"I can't think why it wouldn't," Adam agreed.

"Shelley tells me you're new around here," Ed said, peering at Adam.

"That's right."

"She told me some cock-and-bull story about you having amnesia."

"That's right, too."

"You don't remember anything?"

"I can't recall my real name or my past. I know other things, though."

"Come in where it's cool," Shelley urged. "It's hot enough to fry an egg out here."

They walked across the yard while Shelley and the horse circled to the barn. By the time she rejoined them, Ed had brought out cans of beer. "No glasses?" she scolded her husband.

"This is fine," he told her. "Maya is home folks." He glanced at Adam as if not quite sure what his classification might be.

Adam looked around the room. With its central air-conditioning, the Coopers' place was certainly cooler than the Ranata *hacienda*, but it seemed stiffly formal in comparison. He much preferred the age-mellowed adobe walls to the plasterboard and oak-stained woodwork here. Shelley's furniture, carpet and drapes were all a neutral beige—the sort of color a decorator would suggest to go with any accent. However, Shelley, apparently, had not been innovative enough to add an accent color, and as a result the interior was bland and unexciting.

"It's always so cool here," Maya sighed as she leaned back on a nubby-textured couch and sipped the cold beer.

"You really should air-condition your house," Shelley chided good-naturedly. "This country is too hot to rely on thick walls alone."

"I guess so. Maybe this year."

Ed turned to Adam and said automatically, "What line of work are you in?" Then he realized his faux pas and looked embarrassed.

"I do the Ranata's bookkeeping and help out in the stables," Adam answered smoothly. His eyes fell on some carefully arranged magazines on the table, and suddenly he felt the vertigo of a rush of memory. He recalled a chrome-and-glass table with similar magazines in the same staggered arrangement, and in the background the sound of a sports announcer describing a baseball game. And nothing else.

Slowly he sat forward and shuffled through the magazines, hoping to trigger a continuation of the memory. When nothing else came, frustration welled rapidly within him.

"Adam? Are you okay?"

He glanced up into Maya's troubled eyes. "Fine," he said, belatedly remembering to smile. He gathered the magazines together and stacked them one on top of the other.

"I should go through them and get rid of the old ones," Shelley said, watching him closely. "Ed says my magazines are all over the house."

At last Adam realized what was bothering him. All the magazines in his memory had been the type a woman would buy. So was the coffee table he had seen them on. He sat back and took a deep swallow of beer. Had he known some woman well enough to visit her house and watch a ball game on television? That implied a very close relationship. He tried not to think of the other alternative—that the woman who read the magazincs might be his wife.

"Are you sure you're feeling all right?" Maya persisted. "You look pale."

"It's this heat," Shelley stated. "I've never seen such a dry, hot summer. He probably feels light-headed from the air-conditioning after being out in the sun."

"That's it," Adam agreed. The room was indeed uncomfortably cool.

"All the more reason not to install it," Maya said. "I'm in and out all the time. It would probably give me pneumonia."

"Nonsense. Sickness comes from germs, not temperature differences," Ed told her. He looked back at Adam. "So, do you plan to stay around here?"

"Might as well," Adam said as he put down his beer on the cork coaster. "I have nowhere else to go."

"In a way that's something I envy," Ed mused. "No ties, no responsibilities."

"Ed!" Shelley admonished.

"I didn't mean you, dear." He reached over to pat her hand.

"Sure, you didn't."

Maya got to her feet and handed her beer can back to Ed. "We'd better be going. I have a dozen things to do today."

Shelley walked Maya and Adam to the door, as Ed followed behind them. "Are you going to Ixtapa, Maya?"

"No, I've decided not to go this year."

"You're not?" Shelley sounded almost shocked. "I've never known you to miss it. The Bahamas, maybe?"

"No, I'm staying home."

Shelley glanced at Adam. "I see. Well, we'll miss you there."

"You'll survive," Maya said with a laugh. "Take good care of Lady's Choice—and don't overfeed him," she teased.

When they were back in the truck, Adam said, "You vacation together?"

"Not together, exactly. The Coopers and several of my other friends go to Ixtapa every August. We usually time it so the vacations coincide. That way we have friends available to sightsee and go out with."

"But not this year?"

"I've seen Ixtapa."

"Are you sure it's not having a houseguest that's changed your plans?"

Maya was quiet for a moment. "It's not entirely because of you."

"But partly?"

"I've seen Ixtapa so often that it's like going to Austin. I may break in a new spot. Besides," she added, "I think it all started because Shelley and Ed decided I needed a companion on trips."

"Do you? I should think it would be lonely traveling by yourself."

Maya kept her eyes on the heat-shimmering road. "I've always vacationed alone."

"Then you've never been married?"

"No. I've never been married."

The finality in her voice kept him from pursuing the subject. He was rather surprised, though. He had somehow assumed she was probably divorced. Maya didn't strike him as someone who wouldn't consider marriage. She was too passionate, too giving. For the first time Adam wondered if there might be a secret in her past.

Ocher dust filmed the truck as she parked under the carport beside the barn. Overhead the sun was small but white-hot, as if it were determined to bake the life out of the earth. Maya ran her hand down her sweat-dampened neck and felt perspiration course down her back. "I don't know about you," she said, "but I'm heading for the shower."

A half hour later Adam was changed and cooling off inside the *hacienda*'s sheltering walls. His hair was still slightly damp, and he wondered if he had ever taken so many cold showers before in his life. There was no sign of Maya, so he looked aimlessly through the library. One shelf held a row of picture albums, and after a brief hesitation, he took one down.

Baby Maya cuddled on the lap of a dark-haired woman who must have been her mother, and in another, as a toddler, she clung to the finger of a man Adam decided was her father. There was a snapshot of her on her first pony, wearing a cowboy suit and a broad grin of accomplishment. Adam smiled. Even as a small child Maya had been incredibly beautiful and self-assured.

He replaced the album and took out a newer one. Maya had jumped in age from round childhood to curvaceous womanhood. Surprisingly, her hair was short. These pictures seemed to be of her around late high-school and early college age.

Another face began to appear more and more often in the album—that of a young man with dark brown hair and a chin that Adam thought looked a bit weak. His senior high-school picture appeared to have been touched up, possibly to hide pimply cheeks, and he looked very awkward. In the college photos he appeared more relaxed, engaged in various activities with Maya—a party, their outfits complete with corsage and boutonniere, football games, a bonfire, a fraternity dance.

Then suddenly the boy no longer appeared in the photos with Maya, and her hair was progressively longer—to her collar, her shoulders, then halfway down her back. There were pictures of her with other men, but usually in a group or in front of a show horse. In none of them did he see Maya gazing adoringly at the man or holding his hand.

Slowly Adam closed the album. "I see you found the photos," he heard Maya say behind him. He turned, almost guiltily.

"Yes, I did. You were a beautiful baby."

She crossed the room gracefully, her pale pink dress swirling softly against her silken legs. Taking the album from him, she slid it back into place. "This one is a little more recent that infancy."

"You were beautiful in college, too. I never would have guessed your hair had ever been cut."

She ran her hand over it and tossed it back over her shoulder. "It never will be again."

"Good. I prefer it long. It suits you."

She preceded him to the shady outdoor room, where Lupe had put out a plate of lacy molasses cookies and lemonade. She knew exactly which pictures were in that album, even though she never looked through it these days. Those were of her bad times. The years of losses and disappointments. Years that began with Rick and ended with her parents' deaths.

"There will be a fiesta next month if you're still around. The Coopers are planning a party to celebrate their anniversary."

"Do you want me to be around?" he asked.

She met his eyes directly, "That has to be your decision."

"Is it? What about you? As *patrona* of the Ranata, you have the ultimate say."

"Am I only the *patrona*? Somehow I thought there was more than that between us. Tomás and Javier never push me into the river and kiss me."

"Good," he replied with a smile.

"But you—you don't fit into any slot at all. Neither worker, nor neighbor..." Her silver eyes studied him over the cool glass of lemonade. "Frankly, I'm not too sure what to do with you."

"What would you like to do with me?"

Her eyes slid away, and she swallowed a sip of the icy beverage. "That's not up to me."

"On the contrary. It's entirely up to you." His voice was quiet and held a caress that made her want to look back at him.

"People shouldn't control other people. I'll never tell you to stay or to go. People have to be free to be happy."

"Do they, Maya? Were you happy before I came? You had no encumbrances, no commitments. But then, you still don't, do you?"

She stood and walked to the edge of the shade to gaze out at the pool. She still remembered how lonely she had been and knew she would be devastated if he left. Yet she said firmly, "I don't make demands of people. They come or go as they please."

She didn't realize he had come to stand just behind her until he spoke. "Sometimes you have to ask. You have to make a decision or risk losing something important."

"I make decisions every day," she said with forced lightness. "All the Ranata's activities pass through me."

"Ah, yes. The *patrona*. As aloof and detached as the Sphinx."

Maya looked back, her eyes hurt and troubled, but he had already turned away. She watched him go into the house.

Chapter Seven

Adam followed Maya along the nearly dry creek bed, his interest concentrated on the tightness of her jeans across her rounded derriere rather than on the scenery. Their horses picked their way carefully over the rock-strewn rubble, the reins loose to allow for the animals to correct their stumbles.

"This sure isn't much of a stream," Adam observed. "It's not much more than a damp spot with mud holes."

"It doesn't look like much now because it's a wet-weather creek and we've had a drought all summer. There are no springs to feed it. That's why Javier is moving the cattle to the next pasture, where there's a pond." She pointed up to the high banks that reached well above their heads. "I've seen it almost up to the top there during a flash flood."

"Sure you have."

"It's true. The creek bed is so narrow that there's nowhere for the water to go but up. When the rains come, a wall of water will come roaring through here. That's what cut the creek bed so deep."

Adam looked up at the shallow caves gouged in the walls by rushing water. "In that case, this seems to be a particularly stupid place to ride a horse."

"It will be a few weeks from now, but there's no rain upstream yet, either." She looked up, and not a single cloud could be seen in the pale azure sky. "I'm beginning to wonder if we'll ever get rain again."

Adam silently agreed. A sheen of sweat slicked his body, and his shirt had been damp for hours. Like all the cowboys and Maya, he wore a long-sleeved shirt, not only as protection against the sun's fierce rays, but also as a cooling system. Any breeze at all cooled the soaked shirt and kept him from overheating. His feet, however, felt as if they were baking in the leather boots he wore. Because of the danger of snakebites, no one would even consider leaving the *hacienda* without them.

"Are you sure Javier is down this way?"

"He and the men will be around here somewhere. We'll find them." She turned in the saddle to smile back at him. "By now they'll be glad to see us and the lunch we've brought." She patted the bag of food tied to her saddle.

"If we don't find them soon, I may eat it all myself." He watched as a water moccasin as long as his arm slithered out of the trickle of water and into the underbrush. Despite its wild beauty, the hill country had its drawbacks as well.

"Listen. Hear that?"

The faint sound of whistling and cracking came to them over the still air. Maya nudged her horse up a slope. "They're up here."

Javier and his men were moving one of the herds of Charolais cattle. The huge white cows plodded along stoically between the riders. As Adam watched, Javier whistled, and a small dog darted into the underbrush. Another whistle sent the cow dog scurrying off at a right angle. In a minute a young heifer came trotting out of her hiding place, the panting dog at her heels.

The men without dogs used six-foot whips to flush out the cattle. The whips never touched a hair on the animals, but the loud pops startled the cows out of bushes where a horse and rider couldn't go. When Javier saw Maya he called out an order in Spanish, and his men looked up expectantly. With a whistle he told the wiry dog to keep the herd together. Working with the other canines, the animal obeyed.

"That's some dog," Adam said admiringly to the foreman. "Did you train him?"

"*Sí.* His mama was a fine cow dog, and Charley takes to it natural." The dog heard his name, and his tail wagged happily.

"What breed is he?"

"I don't know. Just dog." Javier pointed to a couple of gray dogs with black spots and yellow markings on their faces. "Those are what we call leopard dogs. I guess they got another name, but I don't know it." He grinned and added, "They always got blue or yellow eyes, though. Must be some kind of breed."

Adam watched the dogs work. The cows were glad to stop walking, and the dogs had only to keep them from wandering back into the brush.

Maya passed the food out to the men, and they
squatted down on their heels to eat. Though a few
leaned back on boulders, no one sat on the ground.
Adam didn't need to ask why. Sitting on the dirt was
inviting a bite from anything from a fire ant to a scor-
pion to a snake. No one wanted anything more tender
than boot leather to make contact with the baked
earth.

Lupe had sent out stacks of sandwiches and several
slabs of cheese and crackers. The men used their own
pocketknives to cut wedges of the cheese and ban-
tered with each other in rapid-fire Spanish. Adam
carried his sandwich over to where Maya was kneel-
ing in the shade of a mesquite and offered her a canteen of water. "Do they all live here on the Ranata?"
he asked.

"Most of them. There's a small Mexican settlement not far from here, and a few live there. The permanent hands usually choose to build an adobe house
down by the river where Javier and the others live. I
have no objections."

Adam studied her. "You really are a *patrona*—in
the old sense, I mean."

"Of course," she said with some surprise. "So was
my mother, and her father was the *patrón* before her,
all the way back to the first Spaniards who settled
here." Her gray eyes followed the undulations of the
stubbled land. "Can you believe some people look at
this and see only mesquite and rocks?"

Adam laughed. "Only those who haven't lived here
for a while." His practiced eye could now detect the
landscape's subtle color changes, could see how the
gnarled cedar twisted like silver driftwood, could ap-

preciate the thousands of tiny yet distinctive wild-flowers that the casual glance would never notice.

A hawk circled overhead, riding an air current that didn't reach earth. Another sat motionless on the upper branch of a dead tree. Keeping to the dense underbrush, a field mouse scampered along in comparative safety. "It's still so untouched," Adam said with wonder. "I wouldn't be surprised to see an Apache ride over the hill."

"Neither would I." She laughed. "Frank Little Buck is around here someplace."

He grinned. "You know what I mean."

"Yes. I love its wildness."

"When I first came here, I couldn't really understand what you meant when you said that you were the Ranata and it was you. Now I do. I can't imagine you in any other setting."

"No? But I go to the city fairly often."

"What city?"

"Houston, of course. San Antonio and Austin are nice, but I'm talking about the big city."

"Of course." He smiled. "How foolish of me." Houston was much larger than the others, but it hadn't occurred to him to think of it as "the big city."

The men finished eating and cleaned up after themselves, tossing scraps of food to the dogs. By the time they tied their canteens to their saddles and Maya rolled up the cotton sacks that had carried the food, nothing was left to indicate that nearly a dozen people had shared a meal there.

"Where to now, *patrona*?" Adam asked as they mounted their horses. "Back to the *hacienda*?"

"Not yet. I have something to show you. Something I've never shared with anyone." With a mysterious smile, she reined her horse away from the herd.

They rode across the rolling hills, and Adam wondered more than once how she found her way. Each outcropping of rock and every twisted tree was unique but not remarkably so, and none of them towered high enough to provide a long-range marker.

Maya reined her buckskin through a narrow space between two boulders that he otherwise would have ridden past. Once Adam was beside her, she caught a cedar limb and drew it across the opening.

"Why are you doing that?"

"You'll see."

The ground sloped sharply downward into a small canyon. The two boulders they had ridden between seemed to be the only entrance.

"My guess is that the local Indians used this as a catch pen and hunting arena," she said. "There's no way out except through those rocks, and it's almost invisible from above unless you know where to look. It would have provided them with a secure place to hide their horses from their enemies. I've found a lot of arrowheads, which means they may have hunted deer in here as well. There's a natural salt lick over by the streambed that would have attracted the deer."

As they rode downhill, Maya pointed to a curious rock formation. "This is Indian Bridge. When I was a girl I imagined that Indian maidens who had been spurned in love leaped off it to their deaths. As an adult, however, I can see that no one in her right mind would use it as a suicide jump, no matter how spurned she might be. All you'd have is a nasty fall and maybe a twisted ankle. Still, it made a good fantasy at the time."

She dismounted and began loosening her horse's saddle. Without asking why, Adam did the same. She laid the saddle to one side, with the horse blanket upside down to dry. The horse sighed as if glad to be rid of the weight, which had left its imprint in a dark area of sweat. Maya unbuckled the bridle and let her horse wander to a clump of grass. Adam watched her last action skeptically. Before he let his horse free, he asked, "Are you sure this is okay? It's a long way back."

"They can't get past the cedar limb blocking the exit. Besides, they'll come to my whistle."

He followed her around the base of the rock bridge and saw her push aside a clump of brush that was covering a crevice in the rocks. Although he was standing several feet away, he could feel cold, clammy air coming from the dark opening.

Maya reached just inside the opening and pulled out a lantern. After shaking it she smiled. "Good. It still has kerosene."

"What are you doing?" he asked as she pulled a packet of matches from her pocket and lit the lantern. "It's just past noon. And why is there a lantern out there, anyway?"

"You'll see." She started to slide through the crevice.

"You aren't going in there!" he exclaimed.

"Sure I am. And so are you. Come on," She had to turn sideways to slip past the rock.

"Wait a minute!"

Adam followed her, but it was a much tighter fit for him. A few feet beyond the opening, they were able to stand erect, and Adam found himself in a cave. The air was musty and considerably cooler, almost cold in comparison to the outside. He shrugged to loosen the back of his moist shirt from his skin. Maya held up the lantern, revealing a huge area with sloping walls. "See?" she said, her voice sounding curiously hollow. "I found this place when I was a girl."

"You came in here all alone? You probably love haunted houses, too."

"Follow me." Moving cautiously, she skirted a pile of rubble, and the lantern showed the way to another opening. Claustrophobic, Adam felt as if the entire hill were about to collapse on them, but he wasn't going to let Maya head off alone.

This opening led down a sloping shaft and into a larger underground room. Maya's face held awe as she lifted the lantern. "Every time I come here I'm struck by the beauty."

The cavern was indeed awesome. It was the size of a football field and almost entirely filled with milky yellow stalactites and stalagmites. Adam agreed that it was beautiful, but it was also very eerie. Every sound they made echoed faintly, and the rock formations seemed like a frozen army poised to attack.

"I call this the ballroom," Maya said. "See? When you swing the lantern the shadows seem to dance."

"I see." He caught her hand to stop the dizzying motion of the lamp.

With Adam close behind, Maya made her way through the maze of rocks to yet another gaping black hole. He swallowed nervously and told himself that claustrophobia was merely a figment of the mind. There was no denying the cave's beauty, and Maya was obviously very familiar with it. Still, he couldn't help thinking of the tons of solid rock piled over their heads.

She led him into the smaller room. "I've never brought anyone in here," she said, her voice echoing spookily against the rock, "but we aren't the first ones. Look at the ceiling." she held the lantern high so he could see the soot deposits on the stone. "Indians also knew about it. They probably used it for ceremonies or something. Look over here."

She led him through a narrow opening. "I moved the rubble aside and found this." She pointed up at the unique ceiling, where slender stalactites protruded like elongated fingers. "They're called soda straws. See how translucent they are?" She looked back at him and decided he looked suitably impressed.

Going back to the ceremonial room, Maya led him to a jumble of bones where the sloping roof met the floor. "Look at them. See? They're what's left of a saber-toothed cat." She looked around in wonder. "There isn't any telling what tribe used this room or how long ago it was. Maybe they even predate the Indians. Otherwise, why would the bones still be here? I've left them untouched because I think of this place as a time capsule. I bring nothing in; I take nothing out."

Adam stared at the large skull with the viciously curving teeth. True, it had been dead since prehistoric times, but if *it* had wandered in, couldn't a live puma do the same? He fought to squelch his growing squeamishness about being trapped underground.

"This way," Maya said.

Adam followed her deeper into the cave. The uneven floor sloped down steeply onto a broad ledge. Overhead the cave soared up to a dome-shaped ceil-

ing. With more even terrain underfoot, Adam felt a
little better—until he heard the rushing sound.

"We're almost there," Maya said, her eyes shining
in anticipation.

He glanced at her uneasily. After the sight of the
dancing shadows in the "ballroom" and the ancient
skull behind them, he wasn't too sure he was ready for
the climax of the adventure.

"This cave was formed by water," she said as they
approached the sound. "You can tell that by the formation. Can't you picture an underground river cut-
ting its way through the rock?"

"Uh-huh."

"I knew you'd like it," she said with satisfaction.
"This cave is very special."

"Yes." He strained to see what lay ahead of the
lantern's glow, but there was only inky blackness.
"What's making that sound?" he asked in what he
hoped was a nonchalant voice.

"You'll see. Watch your step through here. It's
slick."

He needed no second warning. The floor of the cave
below the ledge bristled with sharply pointed stalagmites.

As he steadied himself on a cream-colored stalag-
mite on the ledge, Maya warned, "Try not to touch
them; it turns them dark."

"Right."

He was beginning to wonder if the cave went on
forever. The rushing noise was louder at every turn.
The ledge widened, and as they turned a corner Adam
caught his breath. Ahead of them was a huge waterfall that gushed at least forty feet from an opening in
the rock wall to a green pool at their feet.

"There!" she called out over the torrent. "Isn't it magnificent?"

Adam stared at it, his mouth agape. He couldn't even imagine a sight more awesome. The room was filled with the roar, which seemed to reverberate through his body.

As the light faded he realized Maya was walking away, so he hurried to catch up. Around the next curve he became aware of a faint silvery glow ahead of them, beyond the illumination of the lantern. With each step the glow became brighter. Soon they no longer needed the lantern, and Maya set it down and extinguished it. Taking Adam's hand, she said, "Wait till you see what's around the corner."

When they rounded the last bend, Adam found himself gazing past a deep overhang to a grotto pool, bathed in brilliant sunshine.

"Damn!" he whispered.

"Do you really like it?"

He gazed down at her eager face. "How in the world did you ever find this place?"

"Actually, I found this end first and followed the water in." She pointed to a smooth slide where the subterranean pool overflowed into the grotto. "I brought you in the back way because it's more dramatic. See? There are the horses." She pointed to where the animals were drinking the clear water. "We almost made a circle, the cave opening is just over there."

Now that he knew the cave was open on both ends, Adam felt immeasurably better. "It's beautiful!" he said.

"There are caves throughout this part of the country. This one isn't as big as, say, Natural Bridge Caverns or Inner Space, but it's large enough to be exciting."

"I'll say."

"Some people don't like caves. Can you imagine such a thing?" She pointed to the ledge where a sheet of water ran continuously over the edge into the grotto pool. "See all the ferns on that overhang? It's always cool here, even on days like today. I come here often to get away from the heat. I only wish it were closer to the house." She began unbuttoning her blouse.

"What are you doing?"

"I don't know about you, but I'm going for a swim." She bent and removed her boots and socks.

"I didn't bring my suit."

She avoided his eyes. "Neither did I."

Adam stared at her, not knowing quite what to say.

All at once Maya was afraid she had been too bold, had gone too far. What if Adam didn't share the aching need that consumed her in the lonely nights? Worse still, what if he didn't really find her attractive? After all, he was the one who had pulled back that night the heat lightning had seared the sky above them.

She paused, her blouse half-unbuttoned, and looked at him. Their eyes met, and she tried to read his thoughts and feelings. Adam was a private man; his emotions didn't lie on the surface where just anyone might discern them. She couldn't tell if he was shocked at her suggestion or even appalled that she might be expecting more than a swim.

Trying not to blush, she began to rebutton her blouse. Adam reached out and caught her hands. Again she lifted her eyes to his and found the green depths of his gaze as indecipherable as the hidden pool in the cave. Slowly he drew her hands away and started to unbutton her blouse for her.

His eyes never left hers, and his fingers were sure as he released first one button, then the next. Maya felt as if her heart would flutter out of her chest when his hand grazed her skin. The coolness of the grotto touched her hot flesh as he released each button. Maya made no move to help him, and she didn't let herself look away.

At last he pushed the blouse from her shoulders and tossed it onto a rock. Her lacy white bra cupped her full breasts but did nothing to hide their charms. She could feel her nipples pouting to be touched. Still moving with tantalizing slowness, Adam reached behind her and unhooked the narrow strap of her bra, then eased the flimsy garment off her.

The wind caught Maya's long hair and swept it over one shoulder, half concealing her bared breasts. A muscle tightened in Adam's jaw as if he were struggling to control himself. Slowly his eyes swept over her, memorizing her curves, lingering on her breasts.

Maya released the button at the waist of her jeans and gradually let the zipper slide down to reveal the lace band of her bikini panties. Still Adam hadn't spoken a word, though she knew his eyes hadn't missed a single move she was making. Then she stepped out of her jeans and looked up into his eyes. His desire for her was clearly etched on his features. After only a moment, she quickly slipped off her panties and dove into the turquoise water.

Coolness closed over her head, shutting out the brilliant sun and the tedious heat. Below her in the white sand grew an aquatic forest of ferns and emerald plants. Fish circled curiously but showed no fear as she swam by, the black cloud of her hair floating about her like a cape.

When her head bobbed up, she was near the center of the pool, looking back at Adam. He had removed his boots and shirt and had paused in the act of unfastening his jeans to stare across the water at her. Maya swam to the shallows and waded up until the water circled her hips. Rivulets coursed down her face and neck and dripped from her breasts.

Adam looked as if he had been turned to stone.

Regally Maya lifted her chin, her eyes an open invitation. Adam finished undressing and stood still in the sunlight, letting her smoky eyes study his tall, lean body.

His wind-tousled blond hair and gentle leaf-green eyes were his only boyish attributes, Maya reflected. Hard muscles rippled in his arms and shoulders. His chest was deep, and his belly looked firm. His hips were lean, his legs long and strong. She smiled slightly as she saw proof that he was far more stirred by her than his controlled features would suggest.

She held out her hand to him, the crystal-clear pool did more to enhance her submerged figure than to hide it, well aware that Adam could see as much of her as she could of him.

He walked down the sun-warmed rock and onto the sliver of white sand. As he stepped into the water, he caught her hand and drew her arm around him. His eyes searched hers, and she met them calmly. She wanted him, and she now knew beyond a doubt that he wanted her. Whether he loved her or merely desired her, she didn't know, but she felt enough love for them both.

He bent his head and sensuously licked the droplets from her lips, his breath a whisper against her moist skin. Her lips parted as her breasts grazed his chest and she felt the first touch of his hard maleness. His eyes flickered over her face, and again the muscle ridged in his jaw. Slowly he kissed her, drawing her to him as his arms slid about her.

Maya held him tightly, as if he were her reality and their shared passion her universe. Adam's kisses had made her weak before, but now they robbed her of all willpower, leaving only a need for him that throbbed through her with every pulse.

He raised his head and smiled, then drew her down into the water. Together they swam with long, clean strokes, matching their paces in the silvery-blue water. When they reached the far bank, Adam took her hand and led her out onto the carpet of moss. Behind them hung a tapestry of ferns, and between them and the world was the shimmering veil of the small waterfall.

Maya knelt on the bed of moss, her eyes never leaving Adam's. She had the incredible sensation of her soul touching his, their minds merging and becoming one. Words were unnecessary. Adam lowered himself beside her, and they lay back, their bodies meeting in their first earthly contact, their hearts beating as one. Tiny white flowers wreathed her head, and a small yellow butterfly fluttered by.

This time when Adam kissed her, Maya knew he was hers. No distance of mind or body separated them, and neither wanted to hold anything in reserve. His large hand cupped her breast, and his fingers pearled her beaded nipple to pulsing tautness. Maya moved eagerly beneath him, her hips undulating se-

ductively, promising him everything. But Adam
wouldn't be rushed; like a man who had been offered
paradise, he wanted to sample it all, savor every moment.

Leaving a string of kisses down her neck and over
her shoulder, he licked the dampness from her breast,
then gently drew her nipple into his mouth. As he
sucked and loved it with his lips and tongue, Maya felt
as if she would burst from desire. She arched toward
him and threaded her fingers through the gold of his
hair to guide him to her.

He looked down at her and smiled as she murmured softly. "You like that, my Maya?" His knowing fingers teased her nipples until she moved restlessly
beneath him. "How could I ever have thought you
were distant, cool? You're as hot as the Texas sun."

His hand stroked lower over her slender body and
urged her thighs to part. She opened herself to him,
and he touched the wellspring of her desire.

"Adam," she murmured eagerly. "Love me,
Adam."

"Yes, I'll love you," his deep voice assured her.
"I'll love you until the stars fall from the sky."

He knelt between her legs, and she guided his hips
down until the two of them were one. Maya caught her
breath as Adam filled her. She ran her hands along the
length of his hard back and sides, pressing him tightly
against her as they began to move in love's rhythm.
Slowly they rocked, enjoying the pure pleasure of
being one. Maya had never felt such passion as he was
evoking. He knew just how to move and when to
move, just how to kiss her, just where to touch her to
make her blossom with desire.

Look what we've got for you:

... A FREE compact umbrella
... plus a sampler set of 4 terrific
Silhouette Special Edition® novels,
specially selected by our editors.

... PLUS a surprise mystery gift
that will delight you.

All this just for trying our preview service!

With your trial, you'll get SNEAK PREVIEWS
to 6 new Silhouette Special Edition® novels a
month—before they're available in stores—with
9% off retail on any books you keep (just $2.49
each)—and FREE home delivery besides.

Plus There's More!

You'll also get our newsletter, packed with news of your
favorite authors and upcoming books—FREE! And as a
valued reader, we'll be sending you additional free gifts
from time to time—as a token of our appreciation.

THERE IS NO CATCH. You're not required to buy a single book ever. You may cancel preview service privileges
anytime, if you want. The free gifts are yours anyway. It's
a super-sweet deal if ever there was one. Try us and see!

Get 4 FREE full-length Silhouette Special Edition® novels.

Plus
a handy
compact
umbrella

Plus
a surprise
free gift

▼ PLUS LOTS MORE! MAIL THIS CARD TODAY ▼

Silhouette's Best-Ever "Get Acquainted" Offer

Yes, I'll try the Silhouette preview service under the terms outlined on the opposite page. Send me 4 free Silhouette Special Edition® novels, a free compact umbrella and a free mystery gift.

235 CIL R1W3

PLACE STICKER
FOR 6 FREE GIFTS
HERE

NAME _____

ADDRESS _____ APT. _____

CITY _____

STATE _____ ZIP CODE _____

PRINTED IN U.S.A.

Don't forget...

... Return this card today to receive your 4 free books, free compact umbrella and free mystery gift.

... You will receive books before they're available in stores and at a discount off retail prices.

... No obligation. Keep only the books you want and cancel anytime.

If offer card is missing, write to: Silhouette Books, 901 Fuhrmann Blvd., P.O. Box 1867, Buffalo, NY 14269-1867

"It's as if we've loved before," she whispered. "It's as if I've always known you."

"I know. I feel it, too." He gazed down at her with a primitive hunger that she knew was only for her. "Almost as if you've always been my woman."

He pushed deeply within her as if he were claiming her as his right. Maya moaned with pleasure and met his thrusts with building urgency. Adam met her ardor with an equal measure of his own, and as her passion built, she could see it echoed in the green heat of his eyes.

Smoothly they loved as if each already knew the other's preferences, as if each knew exactly what the other wanted to heighten the exquisiteness of their lovemaking. Maya felt a golden flame leap brightly within her, and she held Adam tightly as it suddenly burst forth like lava to bring her surcease.

When she opened her eyes, he was watching her, a self-satisfied smile on his lips. When her breathing slowed from its ragged pace, he once more started to move inside her. Surprise flickered in the quicksilver of her eyes.

"You asked me to love you, my Maya. Once is not enough for a woman like you." He slid his arm under her waist, making her arch against him. Curving over her, he drew her nipple into his mouth and teased her to even greater passion as his hips began to rotate ever so slightly yet ever so expertly.

Incredibly Maya felt her body respond more quickly than before. Never had she known such ecstasy or such desire to please a man. Running the tip of her tongue along his neck, she gently nipped his skin with her white teeth, then licked the faint saltiness of his skin.

"You're mine, love," he murmured beside her ear as he drew her higher and higher up the mountain of desire. "We belong together. Always."

"Yes," she whispered breathlessly. "Yes."

Again the incredible release thundered through her, and this time she felt him let himself go to ride with her on the waves of satisfaction. Still she held him close, not willing to let him leave the haven of her body. They lay together with their arms and legs intertwined, the moss a cushion for their bodies, the veil of water from the falls keeping their world private and idyllic.

Long moments later, when their senses had expanded back to an awareness of the world about them, Adam plucked one of the tiny white flowers and trailed it over her cheek and lips before placing it in her hair. Gently he touched her face with his fingertips as if he found her as incredible as a miracle. Her lips were dewy and her eyes misty with the echoes of their loving. As he studied her, he wondered if he had been wrong to voice so much of his love for her.

He knew he loved her. He had known it for days, maybe since the first morning when she had come into his room, as sweet as an angel and as seductive as a Siren in her nearly transparent gown. "You intrigue me," he said. "You amaze me."

"You called me your woman," she murmured, rubbing her cheek against the curve of his shoulder.

"Do you mind my having said that?"

"Not if you meant it."

He gazed into her eyes and saw her soul mirrored there, proud and passionate and yearning for real love. Tenderly he cupped her face in his hand, and she moved to kiss his palm before looking back into his eyes. "What do I have to offer a woman like you, my Maya?"

"You have yourself. What else could I ask?"

"How can you be so trusting, so open? Don't you realize the risk you're taking?"

"I'm taking no risk, because I know you. I may not know your background, but I know *you*. I don't give myself lightly, Adam, or casually."

"I know," he said as he gathered her into his arms and held her protectively, almost fiercely. "I know you don't."

Maya wanted to tell him how much she loved him, but she didn't dare. To her the words were almost magical and meant far more than mere caring or desire. She had said them to only one other man, and she had been certain she would never say them again. Now love flowed through her like life itself, demanding to be voiced, but she held herself back. Somehow she knew these words were not held lightly by Adam, either, and she wasn't sure how he would react to hearing her say them. For now, it was enough to feel the delicious sensation of lying in the arms of the man she loved and feeling their bodies still one.

Adam closed his eyes and struggled not to say the words that permeated his entire being. How could he dare proclaim his love for Maya, the regally proud *patrona* of the Ranata? This afternoon of love, stolen from the world of reality, would have to suffice.

But he knew one afternoon of loving Maya would never be enough.

Chapter Eight

The hot road unfurled like a band of molten pewter. To either side were wilted grasses and trees that looked overburdened with the weight of their limp leaves. A few cows moved sluggishly in the yellowing fields, but most huddled together under the scant shade of stunted trees. Maya and Adam, however, were surrounded by the air-conditioned luxury of her car as she raced down the sun-baked highway.

Adam rested his arm on the back of the white glove-leather seat. It had taken him a while to adjust to the speed at which Maya habitually drove, but once he had, he trusted her completely.

Maya slowed as the roadbed dipped and they approached a low bridge, the stream beneath little more than a trickle of water in a baked mud ditch. Pointing out the permanent pole markers on either side of the dip, which were marked off at one-foot intervals in red, Maya cautioned him, "When the rains come, even if they're primarily to the north of us, pay close attention to these markers."

Adam dutifully studied the signs as Maya pointed to the rubble-strewn banks several feet beyond the bridge. "During a flash flood, those are the banks. When the waters rise, they rise fast. Be sure you aren't caught by surprise."

"Can't you go around by a higher bridge?"

"There isn't one. This is the only convenient road to San Antonio and, beyond that, to Houston. Otherwise, you'd have to loop around Austin and come into La Avenida the back way—if those roads were passable, which is unlikely."

"What happens if you're on the other side and can't get home?"

She flashed him a smile. "You have to wait for the water to go down. I can't think of a better excuse for a shopping excursion to Houston."

Adam grinned and pointed to the clock in the car. "If we're going to be in San Antonio in time for my three o'clock appointment, we need to move on."

"There's plenty of time," she said airily. The powerful car pulled forward, the acceleration pressing Adam against the seat.

As they drove, the giant ranches gave way to smaller ones; then the farms appeared. Crossroads communities became a more frequent sight, and once they turned onto Interstate 10, it was only a matter of minutes before the skyline of San Antonio, dominated by the Tower of the Americas on the Hemisfair grounds, appeared.

Maya drove as if she knew San Antonio as intimately as she did the Ranata. After the *rancho*'s quiet,

Adam found the heavy traffic rather unsettling, but Maya skimmed from lane to lane as if rush-hour traffic were an everyday occurrence for her.

The psychiatrist's office was in a steel and glass building located between a Spanish movie theater and a German restaurant. Adam listened patiently while Maya explained to him that, although the Hispanic influence was dominant here, the area just to the north had been settled by German immigrants, many of whom still maintained their own heritage. He didn't know why he already knew that, but he did. No longer did such coincidences seem significant, however, of greater note were those few short, spontaneous recollections he had had. Those, he felt sure, must be strategic links to his identity.

"This way," Maya said when he paused to look around.

They entered the cool, quiet lobby and took a brass elevator to the fifth floor. They found the doctor's office at the end of the hall. The waiting room was decorated in shades of vibrant blue with lighter, powder-blue accents. Every surface that wasn't covered with fabric was of polished aluminum or glass.

Adam went to the receptionist's window and gave his name, then went to sit beside Maya. "I feel out of place here," he whispered. The receptionist glanced at him, and he managed a forced smile.

"There's no need to be nervous," Maya whispered back. "Dr. Ingemar is an old friend of Uncle Garth and also of my father."

"What if he thinks I'm crazy?"

"Nonsense. Just talk to the man, and quit worrying."

"This shouldn't take long. I only have about three weeks to discuss."

Maya gave him an exasperated look, but she had to smile. Despite his teasing, she knew Adam was anxious. "If you're very good, I'll buy you an ice-cream cone when we leave."

"Nope, not a big enough bribe." He leaned closer and said, "How about you instead?"

"That could be arranged," she replied with perfect poise.

Adam laughed softly. To look at Maya in her red silk blouse, white pleated skirt and perfectly tailored navy blazer, who would ever guess that she had such a passionate nature? She wore a long rope of pearls about her neck and matching pearl cluster earrings. Even her hair was twisted into a decorous bun low on the nape of her neck. She looked more like the president of a corporation than the sexy mermaid from their grotto paradise.

Obeying an unseen cue, the receptionist stood and left her cubicle to open a door. "Mr. Russell? If you'll come this way, the doctor will see you now."

Maya gave him an encouraging smile and picked up a copy of *Psychology Today*. Twenty minutes later she was still staring sightlessly at the same page. She could make no sense of the article she was trying to read when all her thoughts were on Adam. She flipped the page and stared at the new one for several more minutes. What were they talking about in there? She was intelligent enough not to expect Adam to return with full knowledge of his past, but she thought he might possibly remember something of importance.

She was disgusted with herself for even thinking it, but she almost hoped he would never remember. As things stood now, he was her lover, her Adam. If he recalled his past, all that might change. Most important of all, he might be someone *else's* Adam. Or Arthur or Asa or Aylworth. That thought brought forth a smile. He could never be an Aylworth.

The door opened, and the man she recognized as Dr. Ingemar motioned for her to come in. "How are you, Maya? Are you keeping Garth busy out there in the boonies?"

"You know Uncle Garth—he's always busy doing something." She followed him down the narrow hallway to the second-to-last door. "Did you find out anything about Adam?"

As though he had not heard her question, the doctor ushered her into a small room that was decorated much like a den. Adam was sitting on a blue chintz couch, and Maya sat down beside him. Adam shrugged at her questioning look, so Maya turned back to the doctor.

Dr. Ingemar sat down in a wing chair and made a steeple of his fingertips. "None of us really expected to have a breakthrough," he said with professional reticence.

"Then you don't know any more than before?" Maya asked, looking from one to the other.

"We have established his probable residence as Texas because of his accent. Since he speaks no German or Spanish, we can probably rule out this immediate area. Even though he might not actually speak it, one would expect him to have picked up a few key words."

"Maybe he forgot them. He looks German."

"So do a lot of people. My guess is that he comes from farther inland, say, around Dallas; but it's just a guess."

"Now what?" Maya felt both relief and frustration. Adam was hers for at least a while longer.

"He could move to San Antonio and start treatment here. I'm sure he could get a job and a place to stay. I could provide him with a letter of explanation as to why he remembers so little, and since he's your friend, I'd be willing to vouch for his integrity. However, I must caution you that the odds that the treatment will lead to a more rapid recovery of his memory than he would have without it are not very good."

"Do you want to do that, Adam?" Maya forced herself to say.

"No. I'm going back to the Ranata."

Dr. Ingemar spread his hands in a helpless gesture. "It's your decision. In my opinion you'll eventually remember everything. The therapy might speed up the process, but as I said, the odds are not great. Once you start getting flashbacks, they'll come faster and faster. At least, that's usually the way it happens. Once in a while a person gets it all back at once, but that's rather rare."

"Is it possible that I may never get my memory back?" Adam asked.

"I won't lie to you. There have been cases where it's taken years, and some have never recovered their memories. It's probable that you won't recall the exact moment you received the blow that caused it, and probably not the few minutes preceding it."

Adam nodded. "I expected you to say that. So it makes sense for me to start building a new life for myself?"

"To an extent. I wouldn't, for instance, commit to a long-term debt, like buying a house, only to find you have house payments on one in Dallas already. And I wouldn't consider marrying. Bigamy is a serious offense, and amnesia is almost impossible to prove to a court's satisfaction."

Maya looked away quickly. Bigamy had an ugly sound to it. Of course, Adam had never once hinted at marriage, and she didn't know if he even truly loved her. All things considered, however, she wasn't so sure she would turn down his proposal. The idea that she could be so foolhardy disturbed her. Besides, she had no right to think of marrying Adam. She had known him only three weeks!

She stood up as Adam did and offered her hand to Dr. Ingemar. "Thank you for seeing him."

"I wish I could have been of more help. Adam, if you change your mind about the therapy, get in touch with me."

"I'll do that."

Adam and Maya went out of the office and down the hall to wait in silence for the elevator. She could feel his tension and didn't know what to say.

At last he said, "I should have asked your opinion about my moving here to San Antonio. I took it for granted that you wouldn't mind my staying on at the Ranata. That was very presumptuous of me."

"No, it wasn't." She looked up at him in surprise. "I never considered that you might leave. You don't want to, do you?"

He gazed down at her, then back at the elevator. "No. I don't want to leave."

The doors glided open, and they stepped inside. As Adam pressed the button he said, "What if I never get my memory back? I can't make you put up with me forever. You have your own life to live."

"If I'm not concerned about it, you shouldn't be, either."

At the lobby level the elevator opened, and they stepped out. "I'll give it to the end of August," Adam said. "If I'm no better by then, I'll leave."

"If you're no better by then, we'll discuss it," she amended.

Maya had called ahead for reservations at the Menger Hotel. A uniformed parking valet took the car away as she and Adam entered the establishment's spacious lobby. The Menger was old but had been restored to reflect its days of glory. Marble columns supported high ceilings accented with white-painted reliefs. The wool rugs were mellowed with age and shone with a dusty rose and gold patina. The back wall opened into an enclosed garden that resembled a jungle. The other walls sported ornately framed paintings of significant events in Texas history and gilt-framed mirrors that must have been as ancient as the hotel itself. The furnishings were all antiques.

"You constantly surprise me," Adam said as they were shown through a second, even older lobby, and up a side flight of stairs. "I expected either a glass-and-steel high rise or an adobe-style inn. Not turn-of-the-century elegance."

"This goes back further than that," she said with a smile. "This is cattle-baron baroque. Actually, I love the antiques. They remind me of my paternal grandmother's house."

Adam looked up three stories to see an enormous crystal chandelier and a frescoed ceiling. "Your granny must have had quite a house."

The bellman met them on the second floor and opened a dark wooden door with a brass plate that read Devon Suite. The high walls were papered in a reproduction of their original covering, and the furniture in the sitting room looked invitingly comfortable. Maya went to the window and drew the curtains aside to view the enclosed garden below.

When the bellman had gone, she took Adam's hand and her eyes sparkled as she said, "Wait until you see the next room." With a flourish, she opened the door.

He chuckled as he stepped in. The room was dominated by a huge oak bed in the shape of a sleigh. A heavy white antique counterpane covered it, and high above was a half canopy that almost touched the ceiling. The massive, carved piece had been polished with great care.

"How in the hell did they get it in here?" he asked as he compared the size of the bed to the opening of the door.

"I have no idea. But don't you love it?"

"This is the most decadent room I've ever seen. Yes, I love it." He looked at the black wallpaper with the yellow and salmon roses. "How on earth do you manage to stay in here all alone?" Instantly he could have bitten his tongue. She had merely said she'd stayed there; she hadn't said she was alone at the time. He frowned at the bed.

"I like to read in bed, and, goodness knows, this one is enough to keep me awake nights," she said lightly. Then she added, "Adam, don't look at me like that. I *do* stay here alone."

"You don't have to explain anything to me. I know you had a life prior to meeting me. No doubt you've had to cancel a few dates rather than leave me at the

Ranata alone. Obviously that day at the grotto wasn't your first time to make love.''

"No, it wasn't," she said coolly. "And I'm pretty sure it wasn't your first time, either."

He gave her a measuring look. "I guess it wasn't."

"I hold all my orgies at a sleazy little joint down the street."

Adam laughed softly. "I was foolish to have said what I did. Will you forgive me?"

"Maybe." Her head was still tilted in the way he thought of as her offended-royalty look.

He went to her and put his arms around her. "You may as well forgive me. There's not enough room in here for a no-holds-barred fight."

She looked unconvinced. "That was still a pretty low remark. Just because you have the advantage of a faulty memory, you can't hold my past against me. Contrary to what you evidently think, I've led a relatively calm life. Besides, for all we really know, this room might be a favorite place for *your* debaucheries."

"I really think I'd remember this room," he said with a grin. "And that bed is absolutely unforgettable."

"We can ask for another suite."

"No way. This bed is growing on me. I've never slept in a sleigh before—I'm sure of that."

"Have you ever made love in one?" she asked, finally giving in to a smile.

"Not yet."

"Then you have another first coming up tonight. But before that," she said as she slid out of his embrace, "we're going to see San Antonio." She put away her blazer, traded her hose and heels for sandals, and swapped the elegant pearls for a belt made of intricate gold chains. "Let's go."

Across the street from the Menger Hotel was the Alamo, historic battle site in Texas's war with Mexico for independence, and a popular tourist attraction, but Maya led him in the other direction, across the street and down a flight of stone steps to a world unto itself.

"Welcome to the Paseo de Rio, the River Walk. Everybody is a little surprised by it at first."

Adam knew that just above them at street level was a snarl of traffic and the rush of frantic people, yet here he stood by a tranquil river with cypresses and cottonwoods mirrored in its calm emerald surface. He could hear no traffic and see no cars. The people on the sidewalks strolled rather than bustled, and fat ducks quacked complacently as they paddled along.

"Next to my secret cave, this is one of my favorite places in all the world," Maya said as they walked along the river-cooled path. "At Christmas the lights in all these trees reflect in the water, and there are carolers singing in English, Spanish and German." She led him under a bridge that he knew must be a busy city street up at ground level.

They sat at a sidewalk café and ordered margaritas and *tortilla* chips. She bent to feed one to a passing pigeon.

"Yet another face of Maya," Adam commented.

She smiled and gave him a *tortilla* chip. "There's a squirrel behind you."

Adam held out the morsel and waited patiently as the squirrel cautiously made its way toward the food, then stopped only inches away, seeming to be assessing the risk of getting close enough to take it. Suddenly, it darted the last few inches, grabbed the chip and, with a flash of its tail, was gone.

When they finished their drinks, they walked along the lazily curving river to the grassy steps of an outside auditorium. Across the water was a stage where young girls in colorful Mexican dresses were dancing to the brassy sounds of a small band.

After the performance ended, they went up the steps, which also served as bleachers, and back to street level. Once again Adam was surprised, however, for instead of returning to the bustle of the city, they seemed to have walked into a tiny and very old Mexican village.

"La Villita," Maya explained. "It was discovered by accident when the city was building the Hemisfair in '68. The way I heard it, it was hidden behind a wall and was almost demolished by mistake. I don't know if that's really accurate, but it makes a good story. Once the builders realized what this area had been, it was restored."

The small houses had been converted to artisan's shops that faced a central quadrangle. The uneven brick patio confirmed the village's age, as did the thick adobe walls of the sand-colored buildings. At one end was a long trellis entirely covered with grape vines. Behind this was a tiny church, its windows tinted a brilliant green by the sunlight filtering through the creeping vines.

"I always come here when I'm in town," Maya said as they left the little church. "It's so peaceful."

The heat was almost too much to bear as they left the village and crossed a busy street to a row of shops that spanned from the street level to the River Walk. The shop they chose to visit held everything from tourist gimmicks to authentic crafts, and watercolors by local artists.

Adam found he enjoyed wandering through the store with Maya. They bought nothing, but he left it feeling he had brought a great deal away with him. Maya was giving him her world, and she was doing it without reservation.

They walked hand in hand along the river as a paddleboat powered by two teenagers splashed by. "Mad dogs, Englishmen—and teenagers," Maya amended with a smile. "All in the heat of the midday sun."

They crossed an arched footbridge and walked by cascading yellow blossoms and a lush river border of huge elephant ears. At the riverboat landing they bought tickets and rode a motor-powered barge down the river.

"It's much larger than I first thought," Adam said as he watched the tiny shops and pocket-size restaurants glide by.

"This river flowed through the original town," she explained. "Of course it's been improved quite a bit from the early days when the settlers came here to wash clothes on the smooth rocks and from the later days when it became not only a muddy disgrace but an actual health hazard. Now it's come into its own and can be graceful again. I like that."

"That sense of rightness is very important to you, isn't it?"

"I like to go with the flow, as they say. Everything has its season and its beauty. It's just a matter of being aware and observing it."

"And every season has its end."

Maya looked over at him and saw sadness in his eyes. "Does it, Adam? Always?"

"Nothing ever stays the same, if it does, it stagnates and dies. Take us, for instance. Right now we're in our spring. There are new discoveries and an intense fascination with each other, and everything is shiny and bright."

"And?" she prompted.

"The next season is summer, one of growing comfort. You'll learn what I like and don't like; I'll learn what makes you smile and frown. After that comes fall, the friction season. That's when I find out that I really enjoy some of the things you detest, and vice versa. Gradually we start doing our own thing to the exclusion of the other, and finally winter is upon us."

"I don't like your seasons. I don't like them at all." She put her hand on his knee; her face showed her concern. "Why do you think it has to be that way?"

"Have you ever seen a constant spring?"

"Just because things change doesn't mean they have to change for the worse! If I thought that awful future was unavoidable, I'd never get involved with anyone."

He was quiet for a while, then said slowly, "Do you know what I think? I think I just found a piece of my past. I think I went through these seasons with someone—right on up to winter. When I was saying all that, I felt as if it had happened to me."

"Why do you suppose you said it in the first place?"

"Because I'm afraid it will happen again." He put his arm around her and held her hand. "Maya, I don't ever want us to grow apart and finally have nothing between us but ice."

"It doesn't have to be like that. My parents were in love all their lives."

He looked unconvinced. "I want to believe you. I want to think our love is as indestructible as Romeo and Juliet's—but with a happier outcome," he added with a strained smile.

"Your life is what you make it," she said firmly. "We aren't puppets dancing at the end of a madman's string. I'll tell you a secret I learned a while back: whatever you put out, you get back. It's simply sowing and reaping. I learned it in expanding my fortune, but it works for love, too."

The boat returned to the dock, and Adam firmly held her hand as she stepped out. "You really believe that? That we can be whatever we want?"

"Of course I do. Especially you—there are no past failures to hold you back." She smiled up at him, and he grinned.

"A philosopher *patrona*. Just what I needed," he teased. "All right, then. I choose eternal spring in our relationship."

"I choose spring, then the comfort of summer when we know the other is reliable and steadfast, then an autumn when we become so much alike that our thoughts and feelings are automatically compatible, then a winter when we can sit by a banked fire and remember all the good times."

"Just don't bank your fire too early," he said with a laugh.

"No, not for a long, long time."

More seriously he said, "Do you think it will be like that for us?"

"The permanence, you mean? I don't know. Who knows what surprises lurk in that noggin of yours?" Her smile faded as she added, "Or whether that other

person you may be remembering is really 'winter' or
if you're just being pessimistic.''

"I don't think I'm pessimistic by nature. That was
such an alien thought—I must have reasoned it all out
before. Therefore I must have finished that relationship—if there was one."

"Look at yourself, Adam," Maya said wryly. "I
don't know if you have someone in your life now, but
anybody as handsome and giving as you are is bound
to have had someone at some time or another." She
was thinking of his lovemaking; a person needed
practice to learn all he knew about pleasing a woman.
Adam had loved before. She was sure of it. And it
would seem that he had loved quite well.

"Hey, what's wrong? You look as if you just lost
your last friend."

"I guess I'm hungry," she said quickly.

"How about this place?" He pointed toward an
Italian restaurant high up on the river bank.

"Nope. We're going to Mi Tiara. It's one of the best
Mexican-food restaurants in the whole state, and it's
right here in San Antonio."

As always, the restaurant was crowded, even though
it was very large. Strolling *mariachis* serenaded the
diners, who were dressed in everything from faded
jeans to sequined gowns. As the musicians sang a love
song, Maya translated it for Adam. "It's very sad,"
she told him. "The poor maiden died of a broken
heart."

"I wonder if that's possible."

"At one time I didn't think so." She watched the
players move to another table and begin a lighter song.

"Do you now?" Adam persisted.

"These days I'm less sure of what I think about a lot of things," she evaded. "What about you?"

"These days I try not to think at all." He watched the musicians and thought that if he had to leave Maya, his heart might shatter irreparably. He wished like hell he could remember whatever had caused him to say those incredibly pessimistic things about life and love on the riverboat. At the time it had seemed like such a familiar progression of thoughts that he was still a little shocked. A divorce, perhaps? Or had he simply been such an extreme pessimist that he had carried his little black cloud everywhere he went?

After they finished eating, they bought *sopaipillas* from the bakery counter in the front of the restaurant and wandered across the way to the market, El Mercado. Its booths of Mexican handicrafts resembled a cross between a flea market and the old shopping area of Nuevo Laredo.

Adam frowned. How had he known about Nuevo Laredo? Yet, in his mind he could see it—dingier than this marketplace, and more confusing, with story upon story piled high in the old building. He shook his head to chase away the uneasy memory.

"Ten dollar then," a merchant said, taking Adam's gesture to be a refusal of his price. "Ten dollar is a steal!" He plopped a carved wooden box into Adam's hand and glared as if the entire transaction was against his better judgment.

Adam fished in his pocket and handed the man ten dollars; then he ceremoniously presented the box to Maya. "To hold all your emeralds and diamonds," he said, "and the bits of your lovers' hearts."

"Thanks." She laughed as she held it in her palm. "There should be plenty of room in it for all that."

Actually, she thought, it was pretty. The wood was golden-hued and had been carved in a latticework design. An enameled rose was set into the lid. Because it had come from Adam, she knew she would treasure it forever.

the ... with ... it was ... The words also
... and had been ... words ... they
... wrote. This may answer him. He felt ... Adam had
...

...

Chapter Nine

Adam twisted and turned, rumpling the covers. His head rolled on the pillow, and a sheen of perspiration slicked his skin. No matter how he moved, his nightmare continued as if in slow motion.

He was in an old-model car, sandwiched between two very unsavory characters. The Mexican on his right kept leaning across him to speak to the Anglo who was driving. Adam felt suffocated and sick and desperately thirsty. When he tried to tell the men this, they merely laughed at him.

Then the car stopped, and he noticed it was almost night, though still light enough to see he was alone with the two men. They were getting out of the car, and Adam realized with a nauseating dread that they were going to kill him. He couldn't make sense of their words, and he felt as if his feet were caught in wet cement, but somehow he was out of the car and standing in the glare from the car's dusty headlights. Still moving as if the action took place underwater, the Anglo grabbed him and pinned his arms behind him, while the Mexican struck him in the stomach, then in the face.

Adam sat bolt upright, his breathing harsh and his body shaking. Wildly he looked around the darkened room for his attackers.

"Adam?" Maya said sleepily. "Adam! What is it?"

"Those two men! I was being beaten to a pulp by the two men I fought at the new barn. The two Javier said were troublemakers."

Maya sat up and put an arm around him. "It's only a nightmare."

"No. No, it wasn't." He got out of bed and went to push aside the curtain. Outside the sky was graying with dawn over the city. "We weren't at the barn. We were on a back road. They had given me a ride and for some reason started beating me up."

"You think it was a memory?"

"Yes, I do. I remember at the barn that the one called Buddy kept looking at me strangely. I think they recognized me!"

"But that doesn't make any sense. If they knew you, why wouldn't they say something?"

"After beating me senseless and leaving me for dead by the side of the road?"

"I guess you're right. Are you positive it was the same two men?"

"I don't know." He sighed as he let the curtain drop back into place. "In my dream it was them. In real life, who knows? It would explain, however, why I was wandering around with bruises and no valuables or identification."

"Yes, it would." She sat on the edge of the bed.

He smiled slightly. "Or maybe that sleigh bed was enough to give me nightmares."

"It didn't seem to inhibit you last night."

With a laugh he pulled her to her feet. "If you still want to get an early start before it gets hot, you'd better get dressed. I don't feel very inhibited right now, either."

Traffic was light as they drove through San Antonio, and the air was still cool from the night. Maya kept thinking of Adam and the unsettling dream, but she didn't know what to do about it. True, those two men had acted suspiciously and had left without even collecting their pay from Javier. Finding them, however, would be almost impossible. Transients rarely gave the same name twice, and neither of the men had particularly distinctive features.

She was so engrossed in her thoughts that she missed her turn and ended up in a residential section. "Adam, check the map and see how to get back to I-10."

He unfolded the city map and pointed to a street ahead. "Turn left here, go three blocks, and that will put us on... Wait! Turn right! Turn right!"

"Right? You said left."

"I know! But turn right."

She managed the turn and stared at him as he leaned forward eagerly. To her this street looked no different from any of the other residential streets they had been on. The houses were of moderate size and well kept, probably the homes of professional people—maybe engineers or young doctors.

"This street!"

"You recognize it?"

"I'm not sure. None of the houses is familiar, but the feel of the place is. Go around the block."

Maya drove slowly up one street and down another. The farther back into the neighborhood they drove, the less prestigious the houses were. "Should I go back to the first street?" she asked.

"No, I must have been mistaken. None of it seemed all that familiar once I looked more closely."

"You must have been reminded of the type of neighborhood and not this particular street."

"That must be it."

"Don't be discouraged," she said, covering his hand with hers. "Your memory seems to be coming back. In due time it will all fall into place."

He nodded and said slowly, "At times I almost hope it doesn't. How's that for crazy?"

She squeezed his hand and started to drive back to the highway. "It's not crazy. Sometimes I'm afraid of it, too. I'm not so sure I can stand to lose you—and I might."

Adam reached across the back of the seat and gently rubbed the nape of her neck. "You aren't going to lose me."

She smiled, but her heart wasn't in it. If he had lived on a street like this one, he must have a family. As a general rule bachelors didn't buy houses like these. She was eager to get back to the Ranata and the illusion of permanence.

The next night a street dance was held in La Avenida to kick off the opening of the town's annual rodeo week. Maya found herself looking forward to it more than she had since her childhood.

By late afternoon she and Adam were strolling through a bustling crowd in the normally sleepy town. Booths had been set up in the alleyways, and the women of La Avenida and the neighboring towns were selling baked goods and various arts and crafts they had created.

Adam held up a wooden goose painted in slick enamel and said, "What do you do with this?"

The woman behind the table said, "You use his beak to hold messages. I have all the companion pieces, too." She pointed at the various duck-shaped towel rings and trivets, duck and duckling doorstops, and a huge duck cookie jar. "Ducks are big sellers this year."

"Wreaths must be big, too," Maya observed as they moved on. The next booth featured door wreaths of every size and description. Wreaths made of twisted grapevines, straw, braided cloth and even chili peppers hung on all the sides of the booth.

As they wandered from booth to booth, Adam bought them corn dogs loaded with mustard and relish. "La Avenida has more life in her tonight than I ever would have expected," he commented.

"Rodeo Week is probably our biggest annual event," Maya said. "You wouldn't know it from seeing things around here on an average day, but many of the people in this area are very civic-minded. We have a festival to celebrate Cinco de Mayo and since it's in May, the flowers are all blooming and the air is still cool. For the Fourth of July we have a giant fireworks display, and at Christmas we have hayrides and caroling."

"I'm looking forward to seeing them."

Maya glanced at him. Would he still be here that long?

"Why do you always do that?"

"What?" she asked.

"You look at me as if you don't believe I mean it whenever I mention being around in the future. Just because I may get my memory back doesn't mean I'm bound to leave you."

"No?"

"And don't talk to me about prior commitments, either. I may not have any personal ones, and jobs can be found anywhere."

"I'm not worried about your finding a job."

"As long as I've been gone, I've probably been fired from whatever I did anyway."

"I said I'm not worried about that."

They walked for a while in strained silence. Finally Maya said, "It's not just that you have amnesia. I'm always afraid of long-term commitments." She narrowed her eyes to watch a small Western band climbing onto a flatbed trailer. "A few years ago I was in love with someone. Rick Jordan. We went to high school together, then college. Everyone, including me, thought we would get married. He proposed and I accepted and everyone was thrilled. Our parents were friends, and La Avenida viewed our union as if it were as inevitable as sunshine."

When she paused, Adam asked gently, "What happened?"

"He ran away with my best friend three days before the wedding."

"Damn!"

"My sentiments exactly. I lost a fiancé and my closest friend in one fell swoop, as they say. A classic jilting. I've tried to tell myself it wouldn't happen again, but way down deep I don't believe it. I loved Rick, and I trusted him completely—Kathy, too. Now here you are, practically a stranger. How am I supposed to believe you when you say you'll be here for me?''

Without answering her question, he murmured, "That explains a lot of things. There hasn't been anyone since Rick?"

"I've dated several men, but never one that I allowed to talk about permanence." She tried to smile, but her pain blocked it. "On the other hand, neither have you, in so many words. To my way of thinking permanence is longer than simply hanging around until Cinco de Mayo."

"It is to me, too. Maya, I can't offer you anything permanent until I uncover my past. You know that. I don't think there is anyone, but I can't say for sure. If there is, I'll . . ."

"Then you'll go back to her. I'm not a home wrecker, Adam. You won't have to choose between us."

The band finished tuning up, and the group's leader called for everyone to gather around. A square-dance club started an exhibition dance, and everyone except Maya and Adam joined in by clapping their hands and tapping their feet to the rhythm.

Adam didn't know of any way to ease Maya's concern. It would do no good to tell her that he couldn't imagine loving another woman as much as he loved her. In the first place, she didn't seem eager to hear it, and in the second, he was still half afraid to say the words. Maya wasn't just anyone; she was the *patrona* of the Ranata. And he was nobody. He didn't want her to think that he might marry her for her money, yet until he had a past to offer her, he couldn't prove otherwise. He looked at her, and when he caught her eye he smiled, hoping to lighten her mood. She answered by squeezing his hand and returning his smile. With the past unknown and the future uncertain, Adam resolved to make the best of the present. It was all they had.

When the exhibition ended and the band struck up "Cotton-eyed Joe," Adam made a mock bow to Maya and offered her his arm.

"You can dance?" she asked.

"Just try to keep up." He led her into the skipping steps and found the dance wasn't as foreign to him as he had expected.

Their steps matched perfectly, and as the music picked up speed they joined three other couples to form a line. Faster and faster the music sped them along, and when it ended Maya collapsed, laughing, into his arms.

"Maybe you're a kicker under that polished exterior," she gasped as she tried to catch her breath. "Whoever would have guessed you could do the Cotton-eyed Joe?"

"I guess I'm a man of many talents." He grinned as the band began a Western waltz.

He spun her away with a masterful touch that surprised her even more. Adam danced effortlessly, as if he were one with the music and the roped-off town square were a palace ballroom. To Maya's mind the waltz was the most romantic of dances, and in Adam's arms the romance had a deeper meaning. He led her in intricate whirls, and she found the steps easy under his guiding arm. Gazing up into his eyes, she forgot the other dancers and lost herself in the unspoken message between them.

When the music ended she was surprised to find all the others had dropped away to watch them dance. She blushed as applause rang out, and she was glad when the music launched into a polka, diverting the attention from them.

She led Adam into the crowd and back into the night. "I need to catch my breath," she said as they walked down the dimly lit street. "Once again you've amazed me."

"A lot of people can dance."

"Not like that. I know just how Cinderella felt at the ball. Maybe you're a prince."

"Or a frog in disguise?"

"No." She laughed. "Not a frog."

"You'd be welcome on my lily pad any time, princess," he said with a leer.

Maya laughed. "I like you, Adam. I really do. You make me happy."

"Good. That's exactly what I want to do."

By the time they returned to the Ranata, Maya had danced until her feet hurt. As soon as she stopped the car in the drive, she pulled off her boots and wiggled her toes in relief. "These were never meant for dancing," she said as she held up the boots.

He came around the car, and before she knew what he was about to do, he scooped her up into his arms.

"Adam! Put me down! What will Lupe think?"

"Lupe has been in bed for hours." He carried her across the yard and onto the back patio, where the tiny Christmas lights welcomed them. He slid open the door with his foot, carried her into the coolness of her bedroom and placed her gently on the serape bed-spread.

"What marvelous service," she said as she collapsed onto the mattress.

"I'm not through yet." He pulled off her socks and began massaging her feet.

Maya moaned with pleasure. "Did you know that the way to a Pisces's heart is through her feet?" She sighed happily.

He chuckled at her obvious enjoyment. "This little piggy went to market..."

"Cut that out—it tickles!" She laughed.

"This little piggy stayed home..."

"Adam!" She reached up and tumbled him back onto the bed, then straddled him to hold him in place.

"This is working out great," he said with a grin. "I'm going to have to remember that pig poems turn you on."

"Adam, you're impossible!"

"No, I'm not. I'm not easy, but I can be tricked."

She laughed as he reached up to unbutton her blouse. "You're incorrigible!"

"That I am. Do you mind?"

"It's one of your more endearing traits."

He removed her blouse and bra and ran his palms over the luscious curves of her breasts. Maya closed her eyes and let her head roll back as she savored the eroticism of his touch. Adam unfastened the thick braid of her hair and let the silky tresses spill over her bare back and breasts. "You're so beautiful," he murmured.

She gazed down at him as he rubbed her hair over her breasts. Love for him pounded through her, and she longed to say the words. Gently she touched his smoothly shaven cheek and ran her fingers over the hard lines of his jaw. "You're a handsome man, Adam. And you're gentle. I like that." She smiled and added, "But not *too* gentle."

He laughed as he tumbled her over beside him on the bed. "You're one hell of a woman, Maya. There's no pretense about you. No subterfuge."

She smiled and unbuttoned his shirt. "Pretenses don't come easily to me," she said, thinking about her love for him. "On the other hand, I don't necessarily say everything that goes through my mind."

"Thank God for that. I can't stand people who do that."

"I know what you mean." She ran her hands over the hard smoothness of his chest. "We can't say everything we think." Otherwise she would not only proclaim her love for him but would plead with him never to leave her and the Ranata.

"My Maya, my woman of mystery."

"Is that really how you see me? Mysterious?" she asked as he kissed the curve of her neck.

"Yes. You're mysterious and exotic and alluring. I never know what to expect from you." He held her face between his hands and said, "I never really know what's going on in your mind. It fascinates me. You remind me of the story about the lady and the tiger, only with you both options are wonderful. I like all your aspects."

"I like you, too," she said, though she meant much more. "You're not exactly an uncomplicated person yourself. A man who can waltz like a dream *and* do the Cotton-eyed Joe is a real enigma."

"You're wearing too many clothes," he complained as he unfastened her pants. "I like these skin tight jeans, but they aren't easy to get off in bed."

Maya raised her hips, and he finished undressing her and then himself while she pulled down the covers. "You know," she said with studied casualness, "I've been thinking. There's no need for you to go back to your room after we make love. You could stay here."

He slid into bed beside her and drew her close. "What would Lupe say? I think she already suspects we aren't exactly platonic friends."

"I don't have to explain my behavior to my maid."

"Ah, yes. The *patrona* rears her head. For a minute, there, I forgot I was dallying with royalty."

"I don't mean to sound high-handed, but I am *patrona*. No one questions my behavior."

"If you're so secure in your noblesse oblige, then why did you jump away from me when Lupe almost caught us kissing this afternoon?"

"That was just a reflex. All right, I'll admit it. I do care what she thinks, but I also dislike sneaking about in my own house. Any way you look at it, right or wrong, we're lovers, and I don't like the idea of your having to leave my room because of what the maid might think."

"I'm not exactly crazy about it, either."

"Then if you want to, I'd like for you to stay here all night." She met his eyes and waited to see if he would show any signs that she was expecting too much.

"There's that look again. Maya, I'm not going to pull away if you get too close. You can trust me. I won't disappear without warning. Hell, you couldn't get rid of me if you tried."

"I won't try." She ran her hand over his narrow hips and up his powerful rib cage to caress his back. "You feel so good lying next to me."

"So do you. You're warm and soft all in the right places."

"Warm, for sure," she said with a laugh. "This is the hottest summer I can remember."

"Me, too," he teased.

Maya laughed softly and lifted her face for his kiss. She enjoyed being his woman, and when he looked at her with that sensuous gleam in his eye, when he held her in the hot nights and made love with her, she could pretend and almost believe that he really did love her. She didn't speak of her own love because her words might force him to tell her how he felt about her. If he didn't love her, she knew she would be heartbroken. So she pressed the length of her body to his and pretended that love words were unnecessary between them.

Adam held her slender body and ached to tell her of his love. Every day he found himself caring for her more.

He could tell by her responses to his kisses and his caresses that she was ready for him, but he waited to prolong their enjoyment. She was so loving and so eager to give as well as to receive. He didn't see how any man in his right mind could ever reject her for another woman. He wanted to break the man in half for having hurt her so deeply, and at the same time he wanted to thank him for not marrying her.

He understood more clearly now what Maya was going through over not knowing his past. What if he had found her, the woman best suited in all the world to be his perfect mate, and she was married to someone else? He also could see now why Maya wouldn't even discuss his choosing her over some unknown wife, even if he was in a bad marriage. Maya had stronger principles than the average person.

He cupped her breast, feeling the nipple tighten beneath his fingers. She was so responsive to his touch. He couldn't imagine loving anyone more, yet he couldn't tell her so, because he had no way of knowing if he was free. Maya, with her iron-clad moral code, wouldn't want to hear the words unless she knew he was free to say them. So he bit back his love words and showed her with his actions.

A film of perspiration slicked their bodies, and he tasted the faint saltiness of her skin. The hot air from the hills blew sultrily across the bed, and even the sheets were warm. Adam licked the beaded nipple and drew it into his mouth as they became one.

Her hot moistness enclosed him, and he struggled to hold himself in check. Although he wanted to satisfy himself with her, he wanted even more to please her. Over the nights and days of their loving he had found that Maya was always able to respond completely several times, and he enjoyed giving her all the pleasure she desired.

They loved and whispered soft words of passion. When Maya was satisfied, Adam let himself reach his own pinnacle, and together they curled together in the wide bed.

"You're so special," Maya said with the contentment of a woman well loved. "I've never known anyone like you."

"In one way my amnesia is almost a blessing," he said as he cradled her head on his shoulder. "I came to you fresh, with no memories of anyone else, no scars from a divorce or a love that went wrong. If I have any bitterness, it's forgotten. It's as if I were born the night I stumbled to your door."

"Your memories are returning. What happens if you recall a bad experience and turn bitter as a result?"

"That won't happen. Knowing you has changed me for the better, however I was before."

"You sound so certain."

"I'm getting to know me better and to see that a loss of memory doesn't mean my personality is necessarily different. I suspect I was just the same before, only with a background."

"In that case, there must be someone who's frantic to find you. I know I would be."

"Would you, Maya?" He held her tenderly and stroked a skein of her midnight hair. "If I were to lose you, I'd tear up heaven and earth until I found you again."

As he held her, cradled in the security of his arms, she relaxed into sleep, and he mused over the complexities of this woman. Beneath her regally impervious exterior was a vulnerable core that wanted to be protected but would fight anyone who presumed to do so. Behind her self-assurance was someone who was as afraid of losing him as he was of losing her. Yet the self-assurance and the regal composure were also real. She curled trustingly against his side, but he knew that trust wasn't given easily. He vowed he would never do anything to damage that trust or to make her silvery eyes cloud with heartache. Whatever his vanished memory held, he wouldn't let Maya be hurt.

When dawn pearled the sky, Adam slipped out of bed and pulled on his jeans. Although he moved silently, she reached out in her sleep for him, and, finding only the indented pillow, she awoke and opened her eyes. "Where are you going?"

He bent to kiss her and said, "You may be the *patrona*, but I'm not the *patrón*. I don't want any gossip going around that could hurt you."

She smiled and watched him leave the room and close the door before she whispered softly, "I love you, Adam."

Chapter Ten

Any news from Joe Bob?" Maya asked as Adam sat down at the patio table.

"None. It seems I sprang full-grown from the earth. Whoever I was, I seem to have been totally forgettable."

"No way." She smiled at him as Lupe brought out their breakfast of *huevos rancheros* and biscuits with butter and honey.

"I think we should make our own inquiries in Houston and Dallas. Joe Bob doesn't strike me as the most efficient man I've ever met."

"Don't let his good-old-boy personality fool you. He's not that bad." She gazed out at the square of sunlight on the tiles. The August sun was already baking the air in spite of the early hour. "It's going to another hot one."

Adam surveyed her with an approving smile. "How do you always manage to look so cool and comfortable in this heat?"

Maya laughed again and spread her napkin over her white cotton skirt. Her blouse was also white, with intricate white embroidery. She wore a narrow gold bangle bracelet and hoop earrings that gave her a Gypsy appearance. "It's all done with sleight of hand. I'm as hot as you are. This summer has convinced me—I'm installing an air conditioner before next year rolls around."

"Why wait?"

"The only person in La Avenida who can install air conditioners is Joe Bob's brother, Jim Ed. Since Jim Ed had a heatstroke a couple of years back, he avoids working in the summer unless it's absolutely necessary."

"Are you serious?"

"Of course. Once you've suffered heatstroke, you're more susceptible to high temperatures. Or maybe you're just more likely to be careful. Anyway, Jim Ed does only repairs—not installations—in the summer. We move at a slower pace here, but it suits us. When you get right down to it, not many things are worth getting into a rush over. The house is hot, but it's been hot every summer for two hundred years—or at least the old part has. I won't melt in the next few weeks, and it's usually cool by October."

Adam shook his head. "I must be used to city life, because it seems to me that if money is no object, you should be able to get whatever you want whenever you want it."

"That's the mark of a city dweller, all right. There also aren't many people with high blood pressure or ulcers around here."

Adam laughed. "Is his name really Jim Ed? Their parents did that to both their sons? Joe Bob and Jim Ed?"

"Double names are common around here. Their sister is Mary Lou."

"Calling them to supper must have been wearing on their parents."

"Once you get used to it, they aren't more difficult than any other two- or three-syllable names."

They finished breakfast and their second cup of Lupe's freshly ground coffee. Maya leaned back in the chair and said, "There's something I want to show you if you feel up to braving the heat. I'm afraid we have to go on horseback."

"It's not another cave, is it?" he asked cautiously.

"No, and it's your own fault that you didn't tell me you have claustrophobia."

"I didn't know until I was in too deep to back out. Literally. Besides, in the end, it was worth it." He grinned at her and winked. They visited the grotto pool often, but after the first trip he had insisted on riding around the outside of the hill instead of going by way of the cave.

"This place is wide open. No claustrophobia possible."

"I'm game. When do we go?"

"Now, before it gets any hotter."

In half an hour Maya had changed into jeans and they were riding into the hills behind the *hacienda*. They forded the shallow stream and angled back into an area Adam had never seen before.

"How do you find your way around? I've been lost for nearly an hour," he said as he glanced at the height of the sun.

"I know every inch of the Ranata. I've ridden over it since I was a child. We're almost there."

In another fifteen minutes Maya pointed to a wall of rocks. "There it is."

Adam rode nearer and saw what appeared to have once been a tiny village beside a lazy creek. The village had long since been deserted, and only the hot wind circled through the remnants of small rock houses.

She dismounted, and they tied their horses in the tall grasses beside the water. Adam felt a strange excitement as he walked down the deserted path that had once been a street. "What is this place?"

"It's called La Acuerdo, the Settlement. The story that has been passed from generation to generation is that La Avenida and La Acuerdo were settled at about the same time by rival brothers of a wealthy Mexican family. Originally both towns prospered, but the year the brother who founded La Acuerdo mysteriously died, the offshoot of the Medina River that supplied their water began to dry up. By the following summer, the water supply for La Acuerdo was too low to support the needs of the people who lived here, so most of them moved to La Avenida. A number of years later, my family acquired what was left of La Acuerdo when the Ranata was formed. My ancestors allowed the old-timers to stay here as long as they chose to do so, but we wouldn't sell them our land, and finally everyone died or moved on."

As Adam looked through the doorways of the roofless houses, a stirring began in him. He felt a surge of interest that went beyond mere curiosity. "Terlingua," he said slowly. "It's like the ghost town of Terlingua out in western Texas. It's about ninety miles from Alpine." He ran his fingers over the stone walls. "This would have been a general store, or something like it. Maybe a trading post. See how it sits a little apart from the houses and has only one large room? There are ruins just like this in Terlingua. Once the cinnabar played out and there was no more mercury to extract, the town was abandoned."

"How do you know all this?" Maya asked.

"And look! See the holes set in the rocks up there? Those were roof supports." He hurried to the next building and pointed at the niches in the wall. "This was a church. Can't you see it, Maya? This village has had no vandals to haul things away. It's a perfect place for an archaeological dig!"

"Archaeology?"

"Sure! Most places have had so many people taking things away and tearing things down that what's left behind is difficult to interpret. And this place is obviously much older than Terlingua. Look how primitive those smaller houses are!"

"I know these ruins are over two hundred years old, because this was pretty well deserted when the original *hacienda* was built. My mother told me La Acuerdo had been built on the site of a much older village. No one knows anything about that earlier settlement."

"Then there may be relics of it here! This may even be a prehistoric site!" He turned to her with great excitement. "Do you realize what this could mean to students of Texas history?"

"It's just an old town," Maya said.

"It's a treasure chest!" He hurried behind the church and stared at the crooked rows of crosses. "A graveyard!"

"Well, you don't think the people would have tossed their dead to the wolves, do you? Of course there's a graveyard." She wasn't so sure she liked what she was seeing and hearing. Adam was speaking of these things as though he were recalling them moment by moment. He had never mentioned any knowledge of ghost towns or archaeology. Maybe his memory was about to return. The idea frightened her.

"It must have been Catholic for it to be in this part of the country and for the church and cemetery to be side by side." He walked among the cairns. "There! Look at the pile of stones marking that grave. That one may have been a suicide, or at least an outcast. See how the grave lies north to south and all the others are east to west? Fascinating!"

Maya stared at him as the knowledge poured from him.

"Look at all the seashells among the stones! Shells were a symbol of the Virgin Mary, or the Magna Mater, and also of Saint James."

"Saint James?"

"He resurrected a drowned man," Adam said absently. "Each mourner would have brought a shell for the grave, even if it were only a freshwater mussel shell. Seashells were brought inland for the purpose of adorning graves." He looked at one of the few remaining wooden crosses. "If there was ever a name painted here, it's long since gone. Names would have been painted, not carved. And no epitaphs. Not for graves this old."

"Adam, you're frightening me!" Maya burst out.

"What?"

"You sound as if you're giving an on-site lecture or something. How do you know all this?"

He stood up slowly and looked back at her. "I don't know."

She smiled shakily. "This opens a new possibility for your career. Maybe you're a grave robber."

With a soft laugh, he came to her. "I don't think that's likely." He gazed around at the town and cemetery. "I feel so drawn to this place!"

"Well, you certainly couldn't have lived here. No one has lived here for several generations."

"Yes, I can see that. But why on earth do I feel so close to it? It's as if I've made some tremendous discovery, but I don't know exactly what it is."

Maya drew a deep breath. She couldn't be so small-minded as to begrudge him his past. Not even if it meant losing him. "Let's walk around and see if anything else comes to you."

They strolled through the open huts, where brush and grass now grew through the packed-earth floors. There were shards of broken pottery, and one niche in a wall held a crude, weather-battered carving of one of the saints. Adam examined everything but touched nothing. Maya spent much more time watching him than looking at the ruins. He moved as if he were in a sacred place and was reluctant to disturb it.

"Did you come here often as a child?"

"If you mean did I disturb anything, no. I walked around a few times, but I seldom came here. When you're up here alone, it has a haunted feeling. An eeriness."

"Good. Then everything really is untouched. Does anyone else know about the place?"

"Javier and some of the men do. Cattle rarely graze here because it's so rocky, so no one comes through unless he's going somewhere else. Like I said, it's spooky to everyone but you."

"Good, good. Maya, would you consider allowing a dig here?"

"Here? I don't know," she said reluctantly. "I hate to disturb it. I mean, it's been here for so long."

"I know. I also know how you are about traditions and not changing the Ranata."

"That makes me sound pretty stuffy!"

"No, no, I don't mean it that way. But a dig would involve people living here for a time."

"You mean right here? In La Acuerdo?"

"They'd probably live in tents and trailers closer to the stream. The excavation might take a year or more."

"Years? Who'd want to live in a tent back here for years?"

"Permanent buildings might disrupt the site. Maya, think about it. There might be information here about the early settlers or an Indian tribe that nobody knows anything about!"

"If it's Indians you're interested in, there was an old burial ground that's much closer to the road than this place."

"An Indian burial ground!"

"I never took you there because there's nothing much to see. Just a few arrowheads and some pottery shards."

"You're sure it's there?"

"Of course. It's even older than this place. Or at least it's older than these buildings."

"No one has dug around in it?"

"Certainly not."

"Maya, this is very important. What tribe was it?"

"I have no idea. All I know is they were long gone before the Mexican people settled here."

"But you know it's there and hasn't been disturbed?"

"I suspect that the settlers of La Acuerdo avoided the burial ground because they were very superstitious back then, and if they hadn't known it was there, we wouldn't, either. Everything has been handed down by word of mouth."

"How about this—let me arrange for a dig at the Indian site first. You can see how it's done and decide then if you're willing to let one proceed at the village." He looked at her eagerly.

"I guess that's fair. I don't have any feeling one way or another for the burial grounds. But remember, I'm not promising anything about La Acuerdo."

"It's a deal."

"Now, how are you going to arrange for this dig?"

"I'll call..." Suddenly Adam's face went blank. He had no idea at all whom to call. "Damn!" He turned from her abruptly and stalked down the steep slope to the creek.

After a brief hesitation, Maya hurried after him. She found him sitting on an outcropping of rocks, scowling at the water. "Adam? What's wrong?"

"I can't remember who to call!" He turned away from her and said tightly, "I can't remember a damned thing that I need to!"

"Adam," she said gently as she sat beside him and put her arms around him. To her surprise, he was trembling. "Adam, that's not true. It's coming back to you. Look at all you told me about the graveyard!

And you knew more about the village than I do. I never knew that first building was the trading post. Your memory is coming back."

"Is it? I can tell Dr. Kadlecek doesn't think so."

"He didn't see you in San Antonio or here in the village. It was as if the more you talked, the more you knew."

He turned to her and put his arms around her, letting her comfort him and give him the sense of security he so desperately needed just then. "I frightened myself when I tried to recall that archaeologist's name. I could see his face, and I could even remember talking to him, but I have no idea who he is or where I met him. Do you know how terrifying that is?"

"No, I don't, but I can empathize with you. I hurt when you hurt, Adam. It's as if we're part of each other."

He held her tightly. "What would I have done if I hadn't found you that night? It scares me to think about it. I might not even be alive now."

Maya knew there was a good chance that he was right, but she said, "Someone else would have found you."

"But it wouldn't have been you."

"I have a feeling we were somehow destined to meet. Maybe your accident was the only way of getting you to the Ranata."

"I don't believe in predestination," he said as he nuzzled her sun-warmed hair. "But I do believe in soul mates, and I'm beginning to think that's what we are."

Her eyes met his, and she saw such love reflected there that she was startled. "Yes," she said slowly. "I think you're right."

The very air between them became charged with unspoken emotions. She knew in her heart that they might both be right. At any rate, what they had between them was undeniable, and she knew that if she didn't do something to break the mood, she was going to blurt out her love for him and possibly ruin it all.

"Lupe made us a lunch," she said quickly. "I hope you're hungry. I know I am." She slid off the rock and went to get the bag of food from her saddle. When she glanced back, Adam was staring at her as if perplexed at her sudden need for food. She peeped into the bag and said, "We're in luck! I see fried chicken."

She used the cotton bag as a tablecloth on the rock as he went to get their canteens. Lupe had thought of everything, even polished apples for dessert. "The way Lupe feeds you, I'm beginning to think she has her eye on you for herself," Maya teased.

"Not and look at Javier the way she does. Do they have any children?"

"Three. They're all grown and married now. I think that's why she despairs of me." She realized what she was saying and pretended to be engrossed in peeling a hard-boiled egg.

"She thinks you should get married?" he probed.

"You know how she is. She thinks all women need someone to protect them." Maya smiled fondly. "The women's liberation movement was wasted on Lupe, I'm afraid."

"Does she have a candidate in mind to be your protector?"

"No. Eat your chicken before an ant does."

Adam seemed to be enjoying her discomfort, for he said, "Maybe Joe Bob or Jim Ed?"

"Not in a million years! Although Joe Bob has tried to date me for years."

"He has?" Adam's teasing smile faded.

"I knew him in school, of course."

"Have you ever dated him?"

"Why, Adam! You sound a bit peeved," she said with great innocence.

"I'm no such thing. Did you date him?"

"We went to the rodeo a time or two. Maybe a few ball games. I really don't remember. Cheese?"

Adam took a slice and frowned at her. "What about this Jim Ed?"

"A couple of movies. Nothing more."

"Why didn't you ever mention any of this before?"

"It didn't seem important. After all, we were only about fourteen at the time, and our parents drove us on these dates." Her laughing eyes met his, and he reluctantly smiled. "Now, you, on the other hand, seem to be making a conquest with Shelley."

"What are you talking about?"

"Well, she drives over at least once a day to tell me how Lady's Choice is doing. Either her phone is out of order or she has some new interest at the Ranata."

"I had noticed she drops by pretty often. Didn't she do that before?"

"Nope. Shelley was born dialing a phone. I've seen her more since I sold her that horse than I did for six weeks prior to that."

"Very interesting. I think I'll ask her about it," he said, struggling to keep a straight face.

"You wouldn't!"

"You're right. I'm teasing you." Then he saw the concern in her eyes and said, "I'm not Rick Jordan, and she isn't another Kathy in my opinion. Shelley might be interested in playing around, but she wouldn't be if she knew about us."

"Us? What's there to know?" Maya asked coolly.

"Don't put that wall up with me. We aren't just buddies, you know."

"Yes," she said softly, "I know."

"My Maya," he sighed. "You're as proud as old Russian royalty. Don't you trust me more than that?"

She looked at him thoughtfully before she finally said, "Yes, I do. That's the problem. I trust you enough to get hurt again. That hasn't happened for me in a long time, and I don't know if I like it."

"I won't break your security eggs."

"My what?" she asked with a laugh.

"Our feelings and dreams and hopes are like eggs—very fragile. We may give one to this friend and maybe two to that one, but we all learn not to give our eggs to someone who's hungry for an omelet."

"What insight. May I quote you?"

"Go ahead and laugh. It's true. You have all your eggs in a basket, and you don't give them to anyone. Oh, you may lend one now and then, but you don't give it for keeps."

"That's not true," she protested, not meeting his eyes.

"Yes, it is. But I'll tell you a secret, honey. If you never give your security eggs away, that basket is going to get pretty heavy."

"Yes, I've noticed that at times."

He scooped up the hard-boiled eggs and put them all in her hands. "There. I've given you all my eggs."

"That's pretty risky, isn't it?"

He shrugged. "I trust you."

"Even with Joe Bob?" she couldn't resist asking.

"Especially with Joe Bob. I was being foolish."

"In that case," she said as she handed the eggs back, "I'm willing to risk giving you mine."

He smiled at her. "Was that so hard?"

"Yes. I'm very fond of hard-boiled eggs."

"In that case, we'll declare these merely symbolic and eat them to seal the bond between us."

"Egg-cellent idea."

Adam groaned. "Very punny."

She laughed and offered him an egg she had just peeled. "I like you a lot. I think you may be the best friend I've ever had."

"Your security eggs are in safe hands, ma'am. I'll protect them with my life, if need be. Fight dragons, swim oceans, that sort of thing."

"I get the feeling you would, too."

"Yes," he said more seriously. "I would."

They finished eating, buried the remains, then walked back through the village. Adam shook his head as if he were perplexed. "Do you suppose I was an archaeologist?"

"Do you know how to actually conduct a dig?"

"No, but I feel as if I've been involved in one somehow. I can't think of what occupations would be on the fringes of that."

"Maybe you had a snack concession."

"You're a big help." He led her into one of the houses and pointed to a rusted iron rod with a disk-shaped end. "See that? It's called a salamander. A person would put the broad end into the fire until it was red-hot and press it onto meat to brown it. This thing here is a trammel. It hung in the fireplace, and the hook could be raised into each of these notches to either boil or simmer something in a pot. Now, why would I know that?"

"Maybe you're a chef, but a poor one who couldn't afford any new utensils?"

"A grave robber is more likely. I have no urge to cook anything more complicated than toast."

"Cooking utensils have no obvious connection with a cemetery, or with archaeology, as far as I can tell."

"I know. And I can tell the differences between Protestant and Catholic graveyards and between, say, those of the Germans and the blacks. Maybe I really am a ghoul."

"Who might be likely to collect antique cooking utensils as a hobby? Never mind. That's a silly question. Besides, who ever heard of a ghoul being so likable?"

"How many do you know?"

"Good point." She wandered to the back of the house and pointed at an oblong metal object with a curve at one end. "What's this?"

"It's pretty rusted, but it's a spokeshave. While the *señora* was heating pots in the kitchen, the *señor* was shaping wagon-wheel spokes."

"Amazing. I'm quite impressed."

"So am I," he said with a grin. "How odd that my only real associations thus far have been with a ghost town and items used a hundred years ago."

"My guess is you may be an archaeologist. Maybe you didn't perform the actual digs, but you know too much about these things for it to be just a casual interest."

"Maybe you're right. I might not remember this archaeologist's name, but I'd know him if I saw him. Maybe I'd even recognize his voice, or he'd know mine. We could call Houston and Dallas and Austin and talk to whomever we can that's associated with archaeology. I don't know just where to start, but it might work. If you haven't changed your mind about showing me the Indian burial ground, I'd like to see it."

Maya had been thinking about those calls and what he might find out, when it dawned on her that he had made a request that required her to respond. Forcing a lightness in her tone, she said, "That's a wonderful idea! Come on, let's ride over to the Indian site and see if you can pick anything up there."

Two hours later they were walking along a mounded hill. Maya searched until she found an arrowhead and held it out to Adam.

"This couldn't be as old as you say if the arrowheads are still on the surface."

"So maybe a later tribe had a battle or built their village here. The legend still says this is a very old place. What do you think? Do you have any insights about this?"

"Only that it would be a good place for a running battle and a bad place for an ambush. I'd pick that gully over there to surprise someone." He looked around critically. "It's pretty exposed for a village site."

"Maybe all Indian chiefs weren't great leaders. Maybe these were led by someone who preferred a nice view to safety."

"Interesting theory," he said with a smile.

"Well, you don't see any Indians still around here, do you?"

He handed the arrowhead back to her. "At any rate, it gives us a reason to call some archaeologists to come out and take a look at it while I take a look at them."

When they were back at the *hacienda*, Adam called information and finally located an archaeologist at the University of Texas in Austin. He dialed the number, even though he hadn't much hope of finding anyone still in his office so late in the day. To his surprise, a man answered. "Hello, I'm calling from the Ranata ranch outside La Avenida. There's an Indian grave-yard here that's supposed to be very old, and I wondered if you'd be interested in looking at it?"

There was a pause; then the man said, "Philip?"

Adam nearly dropped the phone. "What did you call me?" he demanded.

"I'm sorry, for a minute there you sounded like someone I know."

"Oh? What's his name?" He gripped the phone as if it were trying to escape.

"Who's calling, please?"

With a sigh, he said, "Adam Russell."

"Well, Mr. Russell, I could get out there to see the site in, say, the last week of September."

"No earlier?"

"I'm afraid not. I'm flying out tomorrow to a site south of Mexico City, and I won't be back until then."

"I see. And this friend of yours, is he also an archaeologist?"

"No, no." The man laughed. "I should have realized right away you weren't him. He's in a different line of work."

Adam thanked him for his time and hung up.

"What did he say?" Maya demanded eagerly.

"He called me by some name, but he said it so fast and so unexpectedly and there was so much static on the line that I couldn't understand him. You heard me try to get him to repeat it, but he wouldn't. I had to say my name was Adam Russell or he would have thought he was dealing with a nut."

"I guess so." She looked at the date Adam had written on the telephone pad. "September thirtieth. That's still over a month away."

"I guess there's a bright side. If I haven't remembered by then and he shows up and recognizes me, we'll know then. Damn! I should have asked what he looked like!"

"That would be even harder to explain than why you wanted him to repeat that name."

"I guess you're right. Well, I suppose I'll try some others."

As it turned out, however, archaeologists were harder to find than he had hoped, and by the time they gave up, only the one name and date was written on the pad.

"One may be all we need," Maya consoled him. "Especially since he thought he recognized your voice."

"We'll see. September thirtieth seems a long way away."

"Not if it means you may have to leave me then."

Adam pulled her into his embrace and held her close.

Chapter Eleven

Maya drove up to the two-story building and parked nearby before turning to Adam. "Are you sure you're ready for this?"

"As ready as I'll ever be. Are you sure this is the museum? It looks like a jail."

"At one time it was, but the jail moved to a newer facility, and since this building is historic, it was converted into a museum. It's part of our Main Street project. Most of the buildings in town date back to the late 1800s, and there's a lot of interest in restoring them to their original appearance."

"Good idea. That will bring La Avenida some tourist money."

They walked along the elm-lined sidewalk and up the worn cement steps. Slowly they strolled past open "rooms" of life-size vignettes—a Victorian parlor, a 1930s-style kitchen, a Civil War bedroom.

"I don't sense much of anything here," Adam said. "It's interesting, and I like museums, but I don't have that back-home feeling I had at the village."

Adam wandered over to one of the long glass-topped cases lined up in the center of the room. In it was a letter to Thomas Jefferson Rusk from Sam Houston. The sense of immediacy began to build in him. "Maya, come here!"

"What is it?"

"This case of Texas history—it's talking to me. Look over here. There's a trammel similar to the one we saw at the village. That's a noggin beside it," he said as he pointed to a mug carved from wood. "'Noggin' means a block of wood. Early settlers made these because glass was too fragile to carry safely in wagons, and imports were expensive."

She followed him down the rows of familiar items and learned things she had never known about each of them. "Maybe you're a museum curator. I feel as if I'm being taken on a tour or a field trip."

"I'm sorry. I forget you may not be as interested in all this as I am."

"No, that's not it. This museum is one of my favorite places. When they're shorthanded, I do volunteer work here. It's just that your voice changes a bit when you start explaining these things."

"Changes? In what way?"

"I don't know exactly. It becomes more impersonal, as if you were talking to a tour group or a class on a field trip."

He looked around the room. "I could believe I was a museum curator. I feel at home here." He wandered over to another case and frowned. "This letter from Sam Houston to Emmett Walters isn't right."

"What do you mean, 'not right'?"

"Look at the signature on this one, then look at the one on the letter to Thomas Rusk. It's very similar but not identical."

"They look the same to me."

"See this curl on the end? Houston didn't sign his name like that."

Maya looked around to be sure no one could overhear them. "Are you saying this is a forgery?"

"I'm saying it's a fake." He shaded the glass with his hand to make out the words. "Go get someone to open this case."

"I can't do that!"

"Maya, I know what I'm doing. Now go get someone."

She left him trying to read past the glass's glare and found the museum curator, Robert Johnson. "Hello, Mr. Johnson."

"Why, Maya, I didn't see you come in. How are you doing today?"

"I'm just fine. See the tall blond man over by the Sam Houston display? His name is Adam Russell, and he'd like for you to open the case for him."

"Open the Sam Houston case?" Mr. Johnson asked in a shocked voice. "I can't do that."

"I know the request is a bit irregular, but Adam thinks there's something wrong about one of the papers."

"Wrong? Not water in the case!" Mr. Johnson grabbed a ring of keys from his desk drawer and strode across the room. "Last Monday Laree Archer let a little boy bring Coke in here. The boy drank the Coke, but he spilled ice on that very display. We mopped it up, but some of it could have run into the case. Nothing is ruined, is it? It *would* be the Sam Houston case!"

"No, no, Mr. Johnson. It's not water damage." Maya caught up with the man at the display.

"Where! Where's the damaged paper?"

"Mr. Johnson, nothing is damaged. You misunderstood me," Maya said quickly.

"Not damaged? Then why on earth should I open the case?"

Maya caught the man's sleeve to get his full attention. "Mr. Johnson, listen to me for a minute. This is Adam Russell. Adam, I'd like you to meet Mr. Robert Johnson, our museum curator. Mr. Johnson is responsible for having collected a great number of the museum displays," Maya added pointedly.

Adam gave Mr. Johnson a comradely grin, and the man pushed his horn-rimmed glasses farther up on his hooked nose and smiled back. "I thought you should know that this letter from Sam Houston to Emmett Walters is a fake."

Mr. Johnson's smile disappeared abruptly. "A what!"

"See? Look at his signature and the way the *a*'s and *r*'s are made. Sam Houston didn't write like that."

"I can't believe I'm hearing this." Mr. Johnson looked from one to the other and was obviously stunned at their blasphemy. "Not Sam Houston? Of course it is!"

"It's a good forgery, but nevertheless it is one."

"Mr. Russell," he said frostily, "perhaps you don't understand. Emmett Walters was a pillar of our society. He was responsible for turning La Avenida from a trading-post settlement into an actual town. He was made mayor after the signing of the Treaty of Velasco. He certainly wouldn't forge a letter to himself from Sam Houston!"

"I'm sure he was a remarkable man," Adam said stubbornly. "However, Houston didn't write this letter."

"Adam," Maya broke in, "maybe you're wrong. I mean, the handwriting is very similar. Maybe Houston wrote it when he was sick or when he was tired, and that changed his handwriting."

"That's possible," Adam admitted.

Mr. Johnson's thin lips grew thinner as he scented victory.

"However," Adam continued, "the contents are also wrong."

"What?" Mr. Johnson leaned toward the case. "That's impossible!"

"Read the second line of the paragraph about halfway down the page. He's telling Walters that he was baptized the week before in Austin. That's incorrect. He was baptized in Nacogdoches in a house belonging to Adolphus Sterne. The town wanted Houston to go to Washington-on-the-Brazos to represent them at a conference, but in order to be eligible, Houston had to be Catholic."

Mr. Johnson and Maya were both staring at him.

"Check the date, too, and I believe you'll find it's off by a couple of weeks."

"A couple of weeks?" Mr. Johnson repeated.

"He was baptized on Erev Yom Kippur. I remember that because Mr. Sterne, though he was officially Catholic, was really Jewish, and because of the holiday he didn't stand up as Houston's godfather, though his wife was Houston's godmother."

"You're quite an authority on Texas history," Mr. Johnson said coolly.

"So it would seem," Maya agreed.

"Just do me a favor and check the place and date of Houston's baptism," Adam suggested. "If I'm wrong, I'll apologize."

"Well," Mr. Johnson said with a show of great reluctance, "I suppose it wouldn't do any harm. But I can tell you now that Emmett Walters would never do such a thing! I won't be but a few minutes." He frowned and walked away.

"You may have to apologize, you know," Maya said in an undertone. "Mr. Johnson is the best historian in the county. I've never known him to be wrong."

"He is this time."

Maya escorted him to the second floor to show him the re-creation of La Avenida's main street at the time of Texas's struggle for independence. They walked over the board sidewalks beside the illusion of a muddy street, complete with wagons pulled by stuffed horses and mules. The street was lined with authentic-looking buildings—a general store, feed store, barbershop, blacksmith's shop and jail.

As Adam peered through the bars on the front of the jail, he cheerfully said, "Good news. The jail isn't familiar at all."

"Thank goodness for that!"

"You know, it's funny, but I feel such a strong pull to historical things, I'm beginning to believe that I must have worked in a museum."

"I wonder if any museum has a curator missing."

"Do you know how many museums there are in Texas? We can't possibly call them all."

"It was just a thought. I guess our best bet is to wait for that archaeologist at the end of next month and see if he knows you. In the meantime, perhaps a stroll through the library might be of some help."

"There's a library here, too?"

"La Avenida isn't *that* small. True, it's not as big as a city library, but we do have quite a few books. It's worth a try."

As they started to leave, Mr. Johnson came to meet them, a thick history book under his arm. "I'm afraid it's I who must apologize to you, Mr. Russell. Sam Houston was indeed baptized in Nacogdoches, not Austin, and also on the date you mentioned. Thus, the letter in the case is in error and will be removed immediately." To Maya he said, "I just don't understand it. From all accounts Emmett Walters was the best of men!"

"Maybe he didn't mean for the letter to be taken as fact," Adam suggested tactfully. "Walters could have admired Houston so much that he liked the idea of receiving a letter from him. He might even have meant it as a joke."

"Why, yes!" Mr. Johnson said with relief. "That might explain it. I'll replace it with Minnie Crabtree's spectacles and Bible, and maybe no one will ever notice it's gone. There's no point in upsetting the Walters descendants."

"Walters, as in Joe Bob?" Adam asked.

"That's right. Joe Bob, Jim Ed and Mary Lou. They've all been very supportive of us."

Adam and Maya exchanged smiles, then said goodbye to Mr. Johnson and made their way to the museum exit.

Since the library was only a block away, they left the car and walked. The sidewalk was hot beneath the soles of Maya's sandals, and not a breeze was stirring. The sky was pale, and Maya noticed that the birds in the trees were sitting with their wings partially spread to cool their sides. Even in the short walk she felt her blouse cling to her with clammy discomfort. The air-conditioning in the library was such a relief that she sighed blissfully.

"We're putting in an air conditioner if I have to do the work myself," Adam said firmly.

"*We* are?" She looked up at him in surprise at his easy use of the word.

"That's right. We'll go see Jim Ed Walters while we're in town and get our name on the books." Then it dawned on him what he was saying, and he frowned. "I'm sorry, Maya. I didn't mean..."

"I know. Don't apologize." She put her hand on his arm and felt the heat of his body through the fabric. "I like the idea of us being a 'we.'"

Before he could question her, Maya walked briskly into the stacks. Adam followed, since she obviously knew exactly where she was going.

"This is the history section. It's arranged according to country, then state. The Texas books are over there on the back wall. Since there are more of them, they have their own section."

"You have almost this many books at the Ranata," he observed.

"Yes, we do," she agreed, unconsciously using the plural as he had. "A town this size should have a larger library, but I'm afraid my view isn't shared by the majority. Most of the community interest has gone into baseball fields and the like. Those things are important for the children, but people don't play ball all their lives. It's a shame that more of them can't see the value of a well-stocked library.''

Adam nodded his agreement as he went to the Texas section. Pulling out a book at random, he said, ''I've read this book! I know I have. The cover is familiar, and so is the text.'' He grinned at Maya. ''We're getting closer, honey.'' His spontaneous endearment made him hesitate.

She smiled at him and said, ''It's not the first time you've called me that.''

''It's not?''

''You called me honey at the village, too. I like it.''

Adam smiled down at her. ''You're so special.''

''So are you.''

Together they sorted through book after book. Adam showed a knowledge of Texas history that was unusually detailed. He liked pictures of the beach, but he also liked the ones of the pine forests and the mountains of Colorado and the Blue Ridge. He showed no interest in any of the cities, but when he looked at a picture of New York, he asked why King Kong wasn't in sight.

''I think we can omit New York as a possibility,'' she said dryly. ''I doubt if that's the first thought a native would express.''

''I'm positive I'm from Texas. Why else would I know so much about its history? Besides, everyone says my accent is Texan.''

''You're right. Okay, let's consider occupations.'' They went to the section on home improvement. ''You said something about installing the air conditioner yourself. Does this book on home repairs jog any memories?''

He leafed through the book and shook his head. "I could follow these instructions, but they're pretty simple." He took down a book on carpentry and electrical wiring. "Same with these. I think I may be a bit of a handyman when it comes to home fix-up, but I don't have any special pull toward them."

The same was true with plumbing and landscaping. He felt no affinity at all for the law books, accounting or architecture. On the other hand, he was familiar with the card catalogs and could use the library system better than she could.

"You're obviously used to doing some sort of research. Genealogies, maybe?"

"No, that doesn't feel right." He led her back to the section on Texas. "This is my strongest interest, but how could I have earned a living with it?"

"Maybe you were some sort of guide to a reconstructed Western town—like a Texas version of Williamsburg, Virginia."

"I don't think so. Judging from my recent sunburn, I must have worked indoors."

"Maybe this is all a wild-goose chase. There are people who study Texas as fervently as an Anglophile studies Britain. Maybe this is simply a hobby of yours."

"Maybe. As for my job, we may not have hit upon it, or I may have disliked the work and feel no deep connection to it."

"That's possible."

"In which case, I may reevaluate my career when I figure out what it was. I'd rather do something involving Texas history."

"Maybe you could write a book."

Adam looked at her oddly. "Maybe so."

"Why did you look at me that way?"

"I wondered for a minute if I already had." He ran his fingers affectionately down the spines of the books. "Maybe I have. Any of these could be my name. Adams, Anderson, Ashburn, Bailey, Easton. Damn! This is so frustrating!"

"I know, darling. I wish I could do something to fix it."

"You can. You can call me darling again."

Maya blushed as she laughed. "Those words do slip out, don't they?"

He grinned. "Speaking of slipping out, we'd better go. The librarian looks as if she's about to have apoplexy over us talking so much."

"There's nobody else in here, and we're practically whispering." Maya leaned around a shelf and met the elderly woman's disapproving frown. "You're right. I think she's trying to tell us something."

They went back outside, and the heat hit them with such force that Maya found it hard to breathe. "Are you ready to go home?"

"Not until we talk to Jim Ed."

Maya drove them to Jim Ed's house, where he did all his business in his air-conditioned garage. Maya introduced Adam, and Jim Ed nodded. "Joe Bob told me about you. Ain't you the one with no memory?"

"Yes."

Jim Ed shook his head and glanced through the back window to where his wife was baking her skin to the shade and texture of saddle leather. "Can't say I'd mind a little of that amnesia myself," he said as he shook his head dismally. "Well, what can I do for you folks?"

"I'd like to air-condition the Ranata."

"Now, Maya, I know you can afford it, but are you sure you really want to? I mean, I hate to take your money unnecessarily."

"I've thought about it for several years, Jim Ed. I think it's time to do it. This year has been just awful."

"Ain't that the truth! But not all summers are this bad, and you know the Ranata's thick walls are pretty good for keeping it cool." To Adam he explained, "Her daddy had that in mind when he and the wife expanded it back before he died. I told him then that's all he'd need."

"I know, but I really want to put in central air-conditioning," Maya said firmly.

"Central! Now, Maya, you're just throwing your money away there. Put in a couple of window units. You'll save a lot that way."

"Jim Ed, you know I can afford it."

Adam watched the exchange in sheer amazement. "Do you mean you don't want to sell Maya what she wants?"

"Why, sure I do," Jim Ed said in surprise. "I just don't want to see her spend more money than she needs to."

"I don't believe this," Adam murmured.

"It's all right, Adam," Maya said soothingly. "Now, Jim Ed, I'm going to put in central air. Do you want the business, or do I have to find someone from San Antonio to do it?"

"San Antonio!" he yelped. "That would cost you an arm and a leg!" He pulled out a grease-stained order pad and flopped it onto the countertop while he fished in his pocket for a ballpoint pen. "Now, you understand I can't do it until it cools off. You know how I am about the heat."

"I know, and that's fine."

"San Antonio!" Jim Ed muttered as he wrote up the order.

When they were back in the car Adam said, "If I hadn't seen it, I wouldn't have believed it!"

"I told you things move at a different pace here. Everyone in town more or less looks out for everyone else. Jim Ed is like Lupe in that he thinks a single woman needs a man to look after her." She laughed. "He thinks I'm going to use up all my money."

"Are you? I mean, that's awfully personal, I know, but..."

"Not unless the oil field runs dry. Even if it dried up tomorrow, I doubt I could go through all my investments. Nobody makes money ranching these days. I just do that and raise horses for pleasure."

"I see." He wondered suddenly just how rich she really was. For some reason he hadn't considered that.

"Now what's wrong? You sound distant."

"It's not the sort of thing I can ask you."

"Then it must be about money." She sighed. "That's right up there with the taboo questions of how many acres and how much cattle."

"Just tell me this much—do you have enough in your checking account to go, oh, say two months on what's in there now?"

"I'm sure I could go much longer than that. Why, I haven't needed to balance my checkbook in years. Not since gas was discovered on the back acres."

"Gas?"

"It pays better than oil, but it's not nearly as glamorous, so I don't usually talk about it. The money is sent directly to the bank, so I know it's always there. I just siphon off a little from time to time to invest in real estate or some company or other.''

"Oh."

"I thought that would reassure you."

"Maya, don't you realize that, unless I discover I'm J. Paul Getty, you're so far out of my league that we can't ever bridge the gap? No wonder Joe Bob is so sure I'm a con man!''

"Well, you must not be a very good one or you'd remember it," she teased.

"I'm serious! We have nothing in common at all."

"Nonsense." She pulled into a parking space. "We certainly had a lot in common last night.''

"You can't count that."

"I certainly can! If I had known you were going to turn out to be a snob, I'd have left you out in the sun to fry. Come on, let's get some ice cream. I'm buying."

"Why not? You can afford it."

She took his hand, and they went into a quaint little drugstore. Overhead, old-fashioned ceiling fans circled lazily. The floor was covered in black and white tiles like a checkerboard, and along one side was a marble-topped soda fountain.

Maya slid onto a padded stool and smiled at the woman behind the counter. "Hello, Raydene. This is a friend of mine, Adam Russell. Adam, this is Raydene Schultz."

"Glad to meet you," Raydene said cheerfully. "What'll it be?"

"I recommend the strawberry sodas," Maya responded immediately. "There are two scoops of ice cream and a glob of whipped cream on top *and* a cherry.''

''I'm sold.'' He looked around the store and commented, ''I feel as if I've gone back to the fifties.''

''It's part of the Main Street project I mentioned earlier. They still sell modern products, of course, but the atmosphere is much nicer. People have started coming in here more often, like they must have in the fifties. It's a congenial place to share a cup of coffee with friends before work.''

''I can see how it would be.''

Raydene returned with two tall sodas in thick glasses, each with a spoon and a straw. ''We have extra cherries for some reason, so I gave you each two. That delivery boy just can't ever keep an order straight. Last week he left enough eggs to start a hatchery. I put scrambled eggs on special every morning to use them all up, and I still have some left over.''

Adam stirred the bright pink concoction and discovered the ice cream floating beneath the mound of whipped cream. ''It's like a Coke float, only strawberry!'' he exclaimed.

''I don't think I've ever seen you before,'' Raydene said. ''You must be new in town.''

''I am.''

''Hey, are you the one . . . ?''

''That's me.''

''Well, I'll be! Oh, you two excuse me. There's old Mrs. Smith come to pick up her prescription.'' She hurried away to wait on the other customer.

''Is there such a thing as a secret in La Avenida?'' Adam asked.

''A secret? What's that?'' Maya laughed as she winked at him. ''Do you mind?''

"Not really. As a matter of fact, I like it here more and more."

"I'm glad you do."

He sipped the cool soda without comment as he watched Maya's reflection in the mirror behind the counter. He could also see the two women looking at them and talking in low voices. Softly he said to Maya, "I'm putting you in a very awkward position with my living at the Ranata and everyone knowing that I'm the one with no memory, no background. For all I know, that's what those two women are whispering about behind our backs. It's not fair to you."

"Javier lives there, and there's been no talk."

"Javier doesn't live in the *hacienda*, and he's married to Lupe."

"You're a good bookkeeper, and I really need you around the ranch."

"Bookkeepers are easy to find."

"Not around here. And most people wouldn't want to relocate to a place as remote as the Ranata."

"I have to admit it's perfect for me. So much so that I don't want to leave it at all."

"Then don't. *Mi casa es su casa.* Literally."

"Maya, we both know we can't go on like this indefinitely."

"I know, but do we have to rush change? I'm afraid it will come all too soon as it is."

"So am I." He affectionately stroked her hand but was careful that the women behind them couldn't see what he was doing. "We have to remember how things are, though, and not forget to stay prepared."

"Adam, I stay prepared, as you call it, day and night. Every time you smile at me and my heart stops, every time you say my name and I go all quivery inside, I tell myself that this may not last, that you may remember a wife and children at any moment and leave me to be with them. What if you get your memory back and you can't remember all that's happened while you had amnesia? I've read accounts of that happening."

"Not with me. I could never forget you." His intense green eyes spoke the love he couldn't voice.

Maya noticed that Raydene was still gossiping with Mrs. Smith. "From the way Mrs. Smith keeps looking over here, I assume we're still the subject of their conversation."

"Undoubtedly. I should leave for your sake."

"If you have my best interests in mind, you won't go anywhere. I'm telling you that I don't care if there's gossip. It gives people who are bored something to do. This is probably the most exciting thing Mrs. Smith has had to talk about in a long time."

"How can I make you understand?"

"I understand perfectly, Adam. You just can't make me agree."

"You're awfully bullheaded," he commented.

"It must be a result of having a moon in Taurus. I wonder what your astrological chart would show." She smiled slowly as she critically appraised him. "My guess is that you're a combination of Scorpio and Sagittarius. You're sexy, but you care a great deal whether you hurt someone. Whatever it is, I like it, and I don't want you to go." When she saw the perplexed expression on his face, she asked, "Why are you looking at me that way? Does my interest in astrology bother you? It's a science, you know."

"No, no. It's just that you fascinate me—beguile me."

"Good." She put down the price of the sodas and waved at Raydene.

"Y'all come back," Raydene called out from across the store.

As Maya drove them back toward the Ranata, Adam tried to still his troubled mind. Maya had said that she didn't want him to leave, even to protect her reputation. He cared what people must be whispering about her behind her back, but Maya didn't. Or if she did, she must be thinking that her time with him was more important than the wagging tongues.

Maya knew Adam well enough to realize that his contemplative silence meant he was worrying again. She wished she could do something to ease his pain. She wished that he had recovered his memory and had no past to go back to. But that hadn't happened, and it might not. All she could do for now was to comfort him and love him; to tell him of her love, however, would only burden him more. Her father had tried to instill in her the importance of living in the now, and that was all she could do. As her heart went out to him in his anguish, Maya said, "Adam, I know you're sitting over there worrying. Is there anything I can do to help?"

"Yes, there is. You can answer a question for me. Do you really not want me to leave?"

"Don't go. I can't make it any plainer than that."

He wanted to tell her that he would never leave, but he knew he couldn't promise that. After swallowing the lump in his throat, he said, "Thank you, my Maya."

Chapter Twelve

Early September brought neither a release from the oppressive heat nor a single rain shower. Adam, like Maya and the hired hands, often stared up at the brassy sky, willing it to bring some relief.

Maya called Javier in and gave him orders to round up the cattle that were to be sold that fall. "I know we're several weeks early, but we may have to start hauling water soon."

"*Sí, patrona*. The south branch of the creek is not much more than a puddle in most places. I can see the cattle being restless with the heat and dryness."

Maya rubbed her temples and nodded. "I know. I've never seen such a bad year. Bring the steers up to the lot pen, and we'll start hauling them to auction."

As Javier left, Maya turned to Adam. "I hate to sell them so early. Another month would put more pounds on them."

"I don't quite understand how this works. Do you have to sort through the herds for the steers?"

"No, they're all in the south pasture, separate from the other herds. Every spring we have a big roundup to gather them. The bulls are either sent to different herds or sold and new ones bought. That's when we brand, dehorn and vaccinate. The young bulls that aren't good enough for breeding stock are turned into steers and sent to the south pasture to fatten for slaughter. I have another pasture of young bulls that will be sold to other ranches as breeders. The steers are auctioned by weight, so we make more money on a larger animal. They're sold in the fall, so we don't have to feed them through the winter when there's no grass."

"What about the young bulls?"

"We try to sell them in the fall, too, but sometimes we have to wait until a buyer comes along. As breeding stock they bring far more than the beef animals."

She dialed the phone number of the auction barn in town and told the man who answered to be ready to receive the herd of steers the next day. Leaning back on the leather couch, she said, "Well, Adam, you're about to go on your first roundup."

The next morning at daybreak, Maya and Adam rode out of the barn, heading up the work crew. She wore comfortable jeans and had her hair twisted up out of the way beneath a straw Western hat. Even though she wore no makeup or jewelry, Adam still thought she was the prettiest woman he had ever seen.

As they passed the *casitas* behind the *hacienda*, the workers who kept their horses with them at home joined the other riders. Some complained about having to get up so early, but Adam could tell it was in jest. Everyone appeared ready to work, and like Maya and himself, each person carried his own lunch and water for the day. No meal would be sent out at noon during a roundup.

By the time they arrived at the south pasture, the sun was high enough to make the morning uncomfortably hot, though no one mentioned it. The cow dogs trotted obediently beside their masters' horses, ignoring the rabbits that scampered for cover as the riders approached. Adam wondered how the dogs seemed to know this was no ordinary workday.

The south pasture, Adam discovered, was shaped somewhat like a dog's hind leg. As Javier had said, the creek was almost gone, leaving only stagnant water in the deeper holes. Each pasture had its own catch pen and loading chute. By afternoon the trucks and cattle trailers would arrive and begin hauling the animals to La Avenida.

Adam had pictured a roundup like the Hollywood version, but this bore little resemblance to the fantasy. At the back of the pasture, the workers spread out, waiting for Maya's signal to begin. Some of the steers were hiding in the brush, but most of them were simply grazing on the wiry grass. When the riders started toward them, they flicked their ears and headed off in all directions.

Adam was usually in sight of Maya or the men, but frequently he had to double back when a steer broke away and tried to elude him. Quickly he gained a new respect for the horse he had ridden so often. The big bay seemed to have a special sense that told him when a steer would bolt and where one was hiding. At times Adam felt the horse would do as well or better if he weren't sitting on him. Many times the horse whirled so fast and unexpectedly that Adam and the saddle nearly parted company.

He could see Maya riding effortlessly, her supple body staying as firmly on the horse as if they were one. She guided the horse with knee pressure, rarely using the reins at all.

By noon Adam's horse's neck was dark with sweat, and he felt as if his cambric shirt were plastered to his body. He let the horse drink in one of the still pools, and like the others he ate his sandwiches without dismounting.

As they gathered the cattle together, the animals realized something was going on, and more of them tried to make a break for freedom. Adam's horse plunged after the steers, sometimes sliding on his haunches down a stream embankment and leaping up the other side. Adam dodged limbs and vines and felt branches and stickers tear at his shirt. The horse seemed to be tireless; Adam wished he could say the same for himself.

By midafternoon the horse's neck was covered with a foamy lather, and his veins stood out beneath his wet hide. Adam could see Maya on her own sweating horse, and he figured she must be at least as tired as he was. In the brush he could hear Javier and the other men whistling to the dogs or to the cattle, occasionally yelling at a steer in Spanish or English or a combination of both. Adam was surprised to discover that Maya could whistle the way the cowboys did, using her lower lip against her top teeth. By late afternoon he had learned to do it, too.

Once the steers were out of the brush and on open land, they became more docile. Ahead lay the catch pen, and one of the long trailers was already backed into place at the loading chute. A man from one of the trucks ran to open the pen gate, and the cowboys eased the herd of steers into the pen.

Adam rode to the shade of a sweet-gum tree and dismounted. His knees nearly buckled under him, and he held on to the saddle as he flexed life back into them.

Someone had pumped water into the troughs for the horses and cattle, and Adam led his horse over to drink. Javier's dog, Charley, leaped into the horse trough and lapped up his fill before jumping out and flopping down to rest in the shade.

"How are you doing?" Maya asked as she rode over and watered her horse.

"Okay. How about you?" He wasn't about to admit he had aching muscles that he hadn't known even existed. "Aren't you going to get down?"

"Not yet," she said with a smile. "I'll wait until we get back to the *hacienda*." She hooked one leg over the saddle horn to ease her muscles and gazed into the pen.

The steers, all of which looked identical to Adam, were milling about and bawling restlessly. "I can't see any difference in these and the ones in the other pastures," he said.

"Look at their noses. Some are black instead of pink the way a Charolais is supposed to be. Some have weak hindquarters or their backs aren't straight. They all have defects that shouldn't be passed on to offspring."

Adam leaned on the rough planks of the fence and watched as the men who had driven the cattle trucks worked the steers through the loading chute and into the trailer. When the trailer was full, one of them stopped the steers by passing a cedar log through the narrow chute behind the upright posts. The trailer's tailgate was slid into place and fastened, and that trailer was hauled out of the way so another could take its place.

"Let's go home. The men will load the cattle and take them to the auction barn. We've done our part."

When Adam mounted his horse, he saw why Maya had stayed in the saddle. After a brief respite, he was sorer by far than he had been before he let his muscles relax. Javier rode by with Charley at his heels and laughed as he said something to Maya in Spanish.

Maya smiled and translated for Adam, "He wants to know who stole your shirt."

Adam looked down to find his shirt in ribbons from riding under limbs and through brambles. He grinned good-naturedly at Javier. "Next time I'll wear a leather one like my horse did."

Javier threw back his head and laughed, then rode over to his friends to tell them the *gringo* friend of the *patrona* was a good sport after all.

Trying not to wince, Adam rode beside Maya, letting her guide him over the confusing terrain back to the *hacienda*. By the time they reached the barn the horses' sweat had dried and the animals had found the energy to pick up the pace in expectation of the feed they knew was their due.

Maya dismounted and unsaddled her buckskin. Before putting him in one of the stalls that opened into the pasture, she brushed his hide to smooth away the caked sweat and dirt. Over his golden-tan back she could see Adam doing the same for his bay. With a smile she scooped a measure of oats out of the covered metal bin and led the horse into the stall, then pulled off the bridle and poured the oats into the trough.

"I'll make a cowboy out of you yet," she promised when Adam was finished with his horse. She could tell he was as tired as she was, and she could see angry scratches beneath the tears in his shirt. "To the showers with you."

"Do you think I need one?" he teased as he surveyed his grimy hands. "I thought I'd wait for next Saturday."

"Cool, clear water," she said in a tempting voice. "Soft towel, clean sheets."

"I'm convinced."

They went to her room and showered together. Maya gently washed his scratched back and kissed his shoulder between the abrasions. Although she was exhausted, she washed her long hair, soaping the grimy dust away and letting the cold water beat down on top of her head.

"Why is it," Adam said as he rinsed the shampoo from his hair, "that I look as if I tangled with a tiger and no one else does?"

"It's your horse, I'm afraid. Rusty is one of the best cow ponies on the Ranata, but he thinks keeping the cattle moving is more important than the person riding him. I guess I should have given you a less well-trained horse, but you're used to riding him, and I knew he'd be a big help to you."

"Thanks a lot."

"You might have a whole shirt after riding another horse, but you'd be even more tired from having to work the horse as well as the cows."

"No, honey, I can't get more tired."

She towel-dried his back and smoothed ointment on the scratches. "You look nearly as bad as you did the first time I saw you."

"I feel about the same. You folks out here sure know how to have a good time." In spite of his aching muscles he helped Maya blow-dry her hair, then watched as she brushed it into a fall of gleaming black silk.

When they went into the bedroom they saw Lupe had left a tray on the side table. On it was a meal and drinks for two. "Uh-oh. Our secret is out," Maya said.

"She's probably known all along," Adam said. He sat on the bed, then quickly stood up. "I think I'll eat mine from the mantelpiece."

"Poor Adam," Maya said as she tried unsuccessfully to hide her smile. "Next time we'll find you a padded saddle."

"Why aren't you as sore as I am?"

"You get used to it."

"Very stoic."

When they had finished eating, Maya slid the tray outside her door as Adam turned down the bed covers. "I may as well stay in here," he said. "Lupe must know that we sleep together if we shower together."

He lay down and barely suppressed a groan. "I may never be able to get up again."

She lay beside him and said, "I ache all over."

"I couldn't touch you if you fell on me. I'm so tired that seems to make sense."

Maya laughed softly and reached out to hold his hand. "I'm so tired I understood it."

As their muscles unknotted, they slept. Sometime in the night Maya snuggled closer, and when they awoke, she lay in his arms.

"Good morning," he said gently, still groggy from his deep sleep.

Maya closed her eyes again and smiled with contentment. "It's nice to wake up with you beside me."

"It's something I could get used to very easily."

Maya could think of nothing that would please her more than to be able to wake up next to this man every day for the rest of her life. As she stretched and stifled a yawn, gradually awakening, a twinge of apprehension brought her to full alertness. She had no right to think of being with him forever. Suddenly she sat bolt upright and grabbed the alarm clock beside her bed. "We overslept!"

"What?"

"We have to drive into town for the auction."

"How could I forget?" he groaned.

"Cheer up. This is much easier than a roundup." Maya was thankful that this day would be full of activity, for when she was busy, she had no time to think of what the future might bring.

The auction barn was located on the far side of La Avenida, and the parking lot was already full of empty trailers and pickup trucks by the time they got there. Behind the barn were long corridors of small pens with other pens behind them. The inner pens opened into a central aisle that led from a loading chute at one end to the auction arena at the other. Above the aisle was a catwalk where prospective buyers could look down on the pens of tagged animals and jot down their numbers.

Maya and Adam entered the barn by a side door. Inside the air was cooler, but the pungent smell of cows, sawdust, cigarette smoke and leather were almost overpowering. She preceded him up the bleacher-type steps, pausing to speak to people she knew, and they sat on a bench near the top.

The front rows were occupied by the bidders, and after Adam had watched for a while, he learned the subtle signals the bidders used to alert the auctioneer of their intentions. A teenage boy with a buggy whip stood in the thick sawdust of the small arena and saw to it that the cows, brought in in lots of two or three, were kept moving and that the bidders got a chance to see both sides of them.

Adam looked with interest at the people. They were of all sizes and ages, but there was a common thread among them—they were all cattle people. He could tell by the restraint in their movements and the drawl in their speech. The men's faces were brown and seamed from constant exposure to the elements, the degree of leathery lines depending on the number of years they had spent under the sun. The women were less tanned by far and seemed much more extroverted than their men. Cool cotton rather than polyester seemed the fabric of choice for everyone's clothing, and most of the crowd wore scuffed boots that had obviously seen much wear.

"See that man down there in the black felt hat and the blue Western shirt? He's a buyer for a major meat packer. The short man in the red plaid shirt is from the rival company. Between them they buy most of the beef around here." Maya smiled as she added, "Here at the auction barn they act as if they don't know each other, but their wives are cousins, and they eat Sunday dinner together every week.''

"You know what amazes me?" Adam said as he took her hand. "You fit in as well here as you do in every setting. I can't imagine you ill at ease or awkward."

"I rarely am," she said with a laugh. "Dad used to say I never met a stranger."

When the auction was over, Maya collected her money from the cashier and stopped by the bank to deposit it before they drove home.

"Don't forget the Coopers' barbecue is tonight," Maya reminded him.

"Tonight? I forgot all about it."

"We don't have to stay late, but we should go for a while or Shelley and Ed will be hurt."

"As long as I don't have to go on horseback."

"We'll drive. I promise." Maya wished she could avoid going as much as Adam did, but she knew Shelley had planned the party for weeks to celebrate their anniversary.

Maya dressed in an ice-blue dress with a swirling tiered skirt. She fastened on silver hoop earrings and draped an intricate squash-blossom necklace of turquoise and silver around her neck.

When Adam saw her he whistled appreciatively. "You look pretty good all cleaned up!"

"You slick-talking devil," she teased. "You look good, too."

He wore a green-and-gold plaid shirt that complemented his eyes and hair, and tan Western slacks. His hair fell over his forehead in its usual wind-tossed thatch, and his eyes were warm with affection for her.

"Am I dressed right for a barbecue? I wasn't sure what to wear."

"At Shelley's parties you'll see everything from cutoffs to suits and ties. She has an eclectic set of friends."

The party was in full swing when they arrived. There was no need to knock; the front door stood invitingly open. The guests milled about in the large living room, where the air-conditioning unit was futilely trying to cool the air that flowed in the front door and out the rear. Strings of colored lanterns lit the patio area out back and the meticulously pampered lawn. At one side of the open area was a huge brick barbecue pit, where a yearling steer was rotating on a spit. Children dodged and raced around the adults, and a Mexican band vied for dominance over the hubbub of voices.

Shelley hugged Maya, then Adam, as if she hadn't seen them in months, and Ed shook Adam's hand and kissed Maya's cheek. *"Bienvenidos a mi casa,"* he said in welcome. "Go get yourselves a drink. The bar is over there."

Adam asked the bartender for two margaritas and handed one to Maya. They sipped the cold, salty beverage as they watched the band.

When the musicians stopped for a break, Maya said, "Now that it's a little quieter, let me introduce you to some people." She took Adam around the room to meet everyone, and although he tried to remember each name and face, there were so many he became confused. Everyone was having a good time, and no one was any the worse for the booze as yet, though he saw one couple that seemed determined to empty the bar single-handedly.

Before Maya and Adam had finished their drinks, Ed announced the barbecue was done. Bowls of potato salad, pickled cucumbers and tomatoes, ambrosia salad and baked beans sat on one table, a variety of pies and cakes on another. The guests filed by to fill their plates, then found places to sit.

Maya and Adam sat on a black-and-white cowhide rug in the open den and balanced the plates in their laps. All around them the conversation rose and fell, then eddied again.

"I'm thinking about buying me a helicopter," said a big man Adam remembered only as Sam.

"Shoot," a man named Clay replied. "Get a twin-engine Bonanza like the rest of us."

"You need a landing strip for that. My place is as hilly as a camel's back. You know that."

"No, no, you put the hangar by the road and use the pavement for takeoff and landing."

"I never thought of that," Sam admitted thoughtfully.

They launched into a discussion as to which types of planes had wings high enough to clear the tops of road signs and whether or not you could get a ticket for using the road as a runway. Someone commented that Joe Bob would have to catch you first, and everyone broke up with laughter.

"Are they serious about buying airplanes?" Adam asked Maya in an undertone.

"Sure. The Ranata had a plane when my parents were alive. They both had pilot's licenses, but I never particularly wanted to fly. After they died I sold the plane and turned the hangar into a hay barn. It holds a lot of hay!"

"Yes," Adam said slowly, "I can see how it would."

When the conversation swung to motorcycles, Adam found himself listening much more closely. The terms they bandied about and the brand names were familiar, and he recalled the memory he had had of riding one. All at once the memory came back, and this time it didn't fade. He saw the scenery in his mind's eye and remembered the exasperation of being lost on a blacktop road in the back of nowhere.

Again he experienced the motorcycle's sputtering cough before it glided to a halt with its fuel tank empty. He recalled hiding it in some brush beside a rock outcropping and how he had taken particular note of the curiously twisted cedar that marked the place. Scarcely daring to move for fear of disrupting the chain of remembered events, Adam saw himself hitchhiking and being picked up by the disreputable pair.

"Adam? Adam, what's wrong!" Maya whispered.

"I remembered something. I was riding a motorcycle, and I was lost. I ran out of gas and hitched a ride with those two characters who fought with me at the new barn! That's why I was riding with them. They beat me up and robbed me!"

"Are you sure?"

"I'm positive! I hid my motorcycle in the brush by some rocks. There was a cedar growing out of it. If I saw it again I'd recognize it easily." He caught her hand. "Maya, there may be something on the cycle to identify me. The license plates! We can trace me through them!"

An icy dread that started as a prickle on the back of Maya's neck quickly spread through her. Trying not to show her apprehension, she said, "Yes, the license plates on the motorcycle. Where did you leave it?"

His face fell. "I don't know. But it's on a blacktop farm-to-market road, and I'd know the scenery again. We can drive around and look for it."

"We'll start tomorrow," she promised, though her heart wasn't in it. She didn't want him to find the motorcycle, and she felt instantly ashamed of the selfishness behind her thought. He deserved to remember, to know. She had to help him. As reassuringly as she could, she said, "I'm sure we can find it."

She watched him turn back to his plate of barbecue, but her own food now seemed tasteless. She was fairly certain they could find the place. There weren't that many blacktop farm-to-market roads. They were mostly gray concrete or dirt. Because of the large ranches around La Avenida, there weren't many roads in the first place.

Almost transfixed, she watched him, noticing the way the lamp turned his hair to a cap of gold and how his voice deepened with authority when he entered into the men's conversation. All his movements and phrases were so familiar to her now. How could she bear to lose him?

Resolutely she thought of the brighter side. Adam needed to know who he was—that was undeniable. He said he didn't feel as if there was a woman in his life. She still couldn't believe a man like Adam wasn't married, however. But perhaps he had been and was divorced. Clinging to that hope, Maya forced down a lump of potato salad and almost choked.

After they finished eating, everyone wandered back out to the patio, where the *piñata* was hanging. The adults stood back as the youngest of the children was blindfolded and given a small baseball bat. He was told the *piñata* was full of candy, and he had three chances to break it open. Because of his age, he was given a peek first, but his three swings were unsuccessful.

The next to get a turn was a four-year-old boy with hair so blond that he was nicknamed Cotton. He swung valiantly and nicked the leg of the crockery *burro*. Encouraged by his strike, he jumped forward with another blow and lost his balance.

Adam caught the boy before he fell and knelt to right him. The blindfold had slipped down below Cotton's chin, and Adam found himself staring into the boy's innocent eyes.

All at once he saw another boy, very similar to this one in size and coloring but whose eyes were green instead of blue. And another child, a girl, with darker coloring but the same features. And their mother.

Slowly Adam stood, his face pasty white. Judging from the way he remembered these two children crawling familiarly over his lap, he knew they didn't belong to some casual acquaintance. Not when they both had eyes the same color as his. He struggled to remember the woman, but she was a fuzzy image. He vaguely recalled dark blond hair cut close to her head, but worst of all, he remembered her laughing at him and the children and bending down to hug him.

Feeling as if someone had kicked him in the stomach, he said stiffly to Maya, "Let's get out of here."

"What?"

"Let's leave. Now."

She gave him a puzzled look, but they threaded their way through the crowd to say goodbye to Shelley and

Ed. Once they were on their way back to the Ranata, Maya asked, "What's wrong?"

He stared straight ahead into the night and tried to order his thoughts. He found he couldn't tell her. Not when she was concentrating on driving. "We'll talk about it when we get home."

Maya parked in the garage, and they went in the back door. Lupe was already gone, and the house was utterly quiet. Maya tossed her purse onto the glass-topped table and sat down on the white patio couch. "Well? Out with it."

"I had another memory," he said as he sat beside her on the edge of the couch.

"It must have been a dilly. You look as if the world is about to end."

He looked sideways at her as he rested his forearms on his knees. "I remember two kids—a boy about five years old and a girl slightly older."

Maya's breath stuck in her throat. She couldn't speak.

"That's not all. I remember their mother, too."

After a long pause, she got up and moved stiffly to the column that supported the overhang. "Are you saying she's your wife and these are your children?"

"I don't know what to think. The kids were playing in my lap, and she hugged me."

Maya closed her eyes against the tearing pain. After a moment she said, "Then I guess we'd better make a real effort to find that motorcycle."

He came to her and put his arms around her, cradling her back against his chest. "I don't know if it was a recent memory. You've said several times that I might be divorced. The memory may be an old one."

Silently she gazed across the moon-washed patio to where the waterfall tinkled musically into the pool. "There's something you should know, Adam. I love you."

She felt his arms tighten; then he turned her to face him. Even in the darkness she could see the anguish in his eyes. "I love you, Maya. I love you so much, I ache." He pulled her head against his chest and nuzzled his cheek over her hair.

"What do we do now? About us, I mean?"

"What do you want to do? It's up to you, *patrona*. I love you, and I don't feel anything like that for her, whoever she is. But if you want me to move back into the guest room and leave you alone, I will. It's going to be as hard as hell, but I'd do it for you."

"Is that what you want?" she asked.

"No. I want to marry you and never let you out of my sight."

Maya smiled sadly. "How can I be miserable and elated all at once? I feel like a yo-yo."

"It's your decision, darling. What will it be?"

Taking a steadying breath, Maya said, "Let's go to bed, Adam. For tonight you're all mine. Tomorrow we have a motorcycle to find."

Arm in arm they crossed the silvered courtyard.

Chapter Thirteen

All the next day Maya and Adam searched the side roads to the south and east of the Ranata. By late afternoon they were tired, and tension in the car was high.

"Maybe we should have started closer to La Avenida," Adam said.

"I thought it more likely that you came in from Houston, since it's so large, and San Antonio is in this direction, too."

"Damn it, we have to find that motorcycle." He glared out at the cactus-strewn rocks and yellowing weeds. "The license plates could give us all the answers we need."

"Tell me again what you remember."

"I was driving down a narrow, blacktop road. I remember thinking I was lost. There was something about my having taken a fork in the road when I should have gone back to...wherever. I ran out of gas. There was nothing around, so I had to walk. I hid my cycle in a clump of bushes beside a pile of rocks. There was a cedar tree growing out of them. It looked like a big snake, and the only greenery was clumped at the very tip of the main branch."

"That describes several thousand acres around here."

"It's the best I can do," he said testily.

"Okay. Getting mad at each other won't help." After a long pause, Maya said, "What did she look like?"

"Who?"

"You know who. The woman you remembered."

"I didn't see her very clearly. She was about medium size and had short, dark blond hair. It was cut close to her head like a cap."

"What was she wearing?"

"I don't know. Sort of a loose blouse—the kind that hangs down long—and jeans. Tennis shoes. Her blouse was kind of pinkish. It doesn't matter."

"You seem to remember her pretty well for such a vague memory."

"What do you mean by that?" he asked sharply.

"Nothing," she snapped.

He drew a deep breath to calm himself. "Honey, we're both on edge, but having an argument won't solve anything."

"Who's arguing? I'm not arguing."

He tactfully dropped the subject. "We might as well start back. It'll be dark before long, and we don't want to run out of gas out here."

They reached the Ranata by dark, and Maya drove to the hay barn, formerly the airplane hangar, to fill the car from the ranch's gasoline supply. Clouds had piled on the western horizon, but Adam knew by now that they were only idle promises.

As the first of the heat lightning glowed in the larger cloud, Maya replaced the gas nozzle and screwed the tank lid down tightly. "I hope somebody, somewhere, is getting some rain out of that."

"Or at least some wind to stir the air," Adam added as he wiped his damp brow with his handkerchief before getting back into the car.

Maya drove to the house, and Adam opened the door for her. "Let's go for a swim to cool off and relax," he said.

"I'm not sure either is possible." Nevertheless, the idea of a swim was appealing. She put on her watermelon-red bikini and joined Adam by the pool. The water was refreshing as she slid beneath the surface and swam over to the waterfall. "I'm glad you suggested this. I can feel myself starting to unwind."

"So can I." He swam with long, clean strokes down the length of the pool and back to her. Maya watched his lithe movements and wondered how much longer she would have the pleasure of his company.

"You look sad again."

"I was trying to memorize you."

"That's not necessary. I'm not going anywhere."

"Adam, you can't promise me things like that. Not after remembering a family."

"We don't know for sure that I still have the family. Even if I do, I'll have a choice."

"No! I won't hear you talk like that!" She swam away, but he followed her.

"Can you just write off what we have?" he demanded. "I love you, damn it, and I won't give you up! I have a choice—if one needs to be made."

"I won't be part of breaking up a family!"

"How much love could she have for me if she hasn't even reported me missing?"

Maya frowned. He certainly had a point there.

"Honey, you're making yourself miserable by constantly thinking of her. Put her out of your mind until we can find some facts."

"How can you do that?" she demanded in exasperation. "I can't put my thoughts in a closet and then bring them out on command. I have to work this out in my mind, be prepared."

"How much more prepared can you be by worrying yourself sick?"

"I don't know." She was suddenly tired and numbed from worry. She swam to the stone steps and sat on the top one, clasping her knees to her chest. "I don't understand how you can be so logical."

"I guess that's a difference between us." He sat beside her and put his arm around her to pull her back against him.

Maya watched as the ecrie flashes of light from the silent storm clouds were reflected in the upper windows of the older section of the house. Above the corner of the low back wing she could see the clouds approaching. Miserably she said, "I feel as if I'm boiling and storming inside and cold and still on the outside—like those clouds."

"Take it from me, 'cold' is not a good description of you."

"No? A lot of people seem to think so."

"They don't know you as well as I do. Besides, those clouds aren't cold and rigid. They're regal and awe-inspiring and beautiful." He pointed to an arc of lightning that spanned from cloud to cloud.

"I wish it would rain," she said softly as she lay her head on his shoulder. "If it weren't so hot, I wouldn't be so edgy."

"The drought can't last forever."

"That's true of a lot of things," she added wistfully as she gazed up at the vivid display.

Early the next day they drove out to the roads on the Austin side of the ranch. Mile after mile passed in monotonous futility. Maya's nerves were strung as tautly as they had been the day before, and Adam was speaking only when she spoke to him.

"We're going to find that bike if we have to scour every road between here and Austin. Tomorrow we'll try the ones to the west."

Adam studied a state map and frowned. "Austin. Kerrville. Are there any roads around here to Kerrville? Other than I-10?"

"There's the old road that goes up through Bandera and loops down to below San Marcos."

"San Marcos?" Adam sat up a bit straighter. "What is there to see in Bandera?"

She shrugged. "It's not very big. There's the Frontier Times Museum. In February they host a trail ride."

"Frontier Times Museum," he repeated slowly as he rubbed his forehead. "How about Kerrville?"

"It's not far from the Lyndon Johnson ranch."

"Yes! And you'd take Highway 290 from there to Austin!" His fingers moved over the map. "Go down the Bandera road, please."

She cut across a dirt lane that bisected a neighbor's ranch and turned onto the road. Adam leaned forward as she swung onto a blacktop farm-to-market road. "Is this familiar?" Maya asked.

"I can't tell yet. For some reason I feel a strong pull to it." After several miles he pointed to a group of cottonwood trees. "I know those!" In another mile he recognized a curiously painted barn. "I've seen that before, too! Turn around. If I've seen these, I must have been going in the opposite direction. Toward San Marcos, I think."

Maya swung the car around and retraced their route. "There! Turn down that road!" he said in excitement.

"But that's not the way to San Marcos."

"I was lost, remember?"

After a while they came to a fork in the road, and he pointed to the left. "That way."

"You *must* have been lost if you were back in here. This is just a road between ranches. I don't think it's even on the map."

"Slow down. There! See it? The pile of rocks with the cedar growing in them!"

Maya slowed to a stop and stared at the formation. As Adam had said, it was shaped like a twisting snake with only one tuft of green at the top. He jumped out of the car and started for the outcropping of bushes that flanked the rocks. Maya hurried after him, her heart pounding in apprehension.

Adam thrashed among the scrub brush, but the motorcycle wasn't there. He glared around him angrily. "This is the place! I know it!"

"Maybe you're mistaken. You know how often you've said the country all looks alike to you. There must be thousands of cedar trees growing out of rocks."

"Not that look exactly like this one. I tell you, this is the place!"

"Then, where's the motorcycle?" she asked reasonably.

He knelt and touched a fresh scar on the rock's surface. "This is where I lowered the kickstand. Someone stole my damned motorcycle!"

"Stole it?"

He tightened his mouth to contain the helpless frustration that made him so angry. "Who would use this road?"

"Dozens of people I guess. Mainly hired hands on this ranch or a neighboring one. Maybe somebody who knows this is a shortcut to Highway 46."

"It was so hot, I wasn't thinking clearly. I must not have hidden the bike as well as I thought."

"I can see my car from here. I suppose someone could see a motorcycle, especially if the sunlight glinted off it."

Adam ran his fingers through his hair as fury built within him. "We came so close! So damned close!"

Maya's heart went out to him. She could feel his frustration and could well imagine the turmoil he must be going through. They had both put so much stock in finding the motorcycle and tracing the plates. "Almost everyone drives a pickup. Stealing it would be no problem, even if it was out of gas."

"I know!" he snapped. "That's fairly obvious."

"You needn't bite my head off."

"I'm sorry! Now, give me a minute to think."

She glared at him. "I know you're upset, but there's no reason to take it out on me. So you have to wait a few weeks to get more of your memory back. I don't see why—"

"You don't see why that upsets me?" he finished for her. "I should think anyone could understand that!"

"Please don't shout at me," she begged, her own voice rising in frustration. "I'm as eager as you are to find out that woman's name!"

"Will you stop bringing her up every time I turn around?" he roared.

"Yes," she said with frigid anger. "I'll stop bringing her up. I'll even stop speaking to you!" She strode off to the car and hardly waited until he was in the seat before she spun away.

Under normal circumstances Adam found Maya's driving habits unsettling, but now she was terrifying. He bit back the admonitions that were on the tip of his tongue, knowing anything he said would only anger her more. When they screeched to a stop at the Ranata and she flung herself out of the car, Adam decided to wait a few minutes before going in after her. She obviously needed some time to cool off. Still, he didn't want to wait long. He had never seen Maya this angry, and he was becoming concerned.

He entered the house and called to her, but she didn't answer. As he looked from room to room his anxiety built. Where could she have gone? he worried. As he neared the kitchen, almost yelling Maya's name, Lupe hurried out to meet him. Her face showed her concern, as well. As she wiped her hands on her white apron, she addressed him excitedly in Spanish.

"Lupe, say it in English," Adam commanded, but she must have been too upset to translate her thoughts. However, she pushed him toward the back door and pointed outside saying, *"Patrona! Patrona!"*

Growling in exasperation, Adam strode out of the *hacienda* and down to the barn. As he had feared, her horse was gone. "Tomás! Tomás Salazar!" When the head groom came running in from the tack room, Adam said, "Where's the *patrona*?"

"She get her horse and ride off. Something is wrong?"

"Which way did she go?"

Tomás pointed toward the west.

Adam hurriedly saddled the bay and headed him out of the barn at a gallop. His Maya was out there somewhere, angry and hurt because of his temper, and he had a pretty good idea where she might have gone.

Before long he topped a high hill and reined his horse between the cleft in the rocks, then headed toward the lagoon end of Maya's secret cave. As he had expected, her horse was there, but she was nowhere in sight. Taking a deep breath, he climbed the slope to the large rock that spilled a sheet of water into the lagoon. Ahead yawned the black cave. He could feel the clammy air and smell the mustiness of ancient earth.

He called out to her, but his words couldn't compete with the roar of the underground waterfall. There was only one thing to do. He had to go inside. Taking a deep breath, he plunged into the darkness. Without a lantern the cave seemed blacker and the waterfall louder than before. He waited for his eyes to adjust to the faint light that pierced the opening. Finally he saw the lower cascade of the waterfall, its source lost in the solid blackness far above his head.

Adam touched the slick wall and kept his hand there as he considered his next move. He remembered the ledge as being wide and smooth, but there was no telling how deep the water was in the underground pool. If he fell in, he knew he might be pulled down by the undertow of the waterfall. The thought wasn't reassuring.

As he inched his way forward, he found the clammy press of the cave's stale, damp air even more distressing in the dark. Only the belief that Maya was alone in there and needed him kept him going. He felt his way around a bend in the rock, telling himself the cave wasn't likely to collapse and that saber-toothed cats had left it thousands of years ago. Logic didn't help a great deal against his claustrophobia, but the thought of Maya did. She needed him, and he had to find her.

After turning another curve he saw a glimmer of light. Hope surged up in him, and he found it easier to go on. A few yards farther on, he saw her in the ancient ritual chamber, the lamp glowing beside her. She sat cross-legged, like an Indian, her hair loose and flowing. She looked more as if she were a link to a forgotten tribe than the *patrona* of the Ranata.

She heard his boot strike a stone and jerked her head up. In the lamplight Adam could see the streaks of tears on her cheeks. She stared silently at him as he came nearer. "You came here?" she said at last. "Into the cave?"

He sat down beside her but didn't touch her. "I wouldn't leave you to cry in here by yourself."

Again she had the strange but pleasant feeling that he could sense her thoughts. "How did you know I was crying?"

He reached up and touched her damp cheeks. "I'm sorry I snapped at you. We're both on edge over all this. Will you forgive me?"

She nodded. "I'm angry with myself. I knew you were upset, and I was thoughtless."

He gathered her into his arms and held her. She breathed deep of the scent of soap and sun-warmed grasses that always clung to his clothes. "Somehow we're going to get through this. I'm just so very much afraid of losing you."

"I know. I'm at least that afraid of losing you. I love you, Maya."

"I love you, Adam."

"You know, you pick the worst places I've ever seen to hide and lick your wounds."

She laughed despite herself. "I never thought you'd look for me in here."

"Honey, don't ever hide from me. Yell at me, sulk, do anything you please, but don't ever hide from me."

"You don't understand. I'm crying. I hate to cry. It's so... weak."

"No, it's not." He lifted her hand and put it on his cheek. She was surprised to feel tears. "It's not weak to cry," he said gently.

In wonder she drew back and looked at him. He, too, had been crying. "Why?" she said, touching a tear that clung to his eyelashes.

"Because we fought. Because you ran from me. Because I found you here, hiding in a cave, crying. I love you, Maya. When you're unhappy, I am, too."

She kissed him and got to her feet. "Let's go Adam. I don't need to hide anymore."

The next day, with renewed strength and resolve, they drove to Austin. Adam recognized the capitol building at once. "That proves nothing, though," he pointed out. "Most capitol buildings look more or less alike, and I must have been here at one time or another."

They drove through the downtown areas, and Adam found himself becoming excited despite not wanting to get his hopes up. "I recognize these stores. Turn here. It goes to the park. Turn into the next block," he said later. "This goes to the university."

When they reached the campus and parked, he got out. Maya came around the car to stand beside him. "Anything?" she asked.

He shook his head, but his expression was confused. "Yes and no. It's like trying to recall a name that you haven't heard lately. You're positive that you know it, but you can't bring it to the surface."

"That must be just awful." She put her hand on his arm. "If I could, I'd trade places with you."

"Careful what you ask for," he said wryly. "You might get it."

"If it would make you happy and give you back your past, I'd take it willingly."

Adam put his arm around her. "I love you, too."

They walked up a sidewalk and looked at the buildings, but Adam again shook his head. "I know this place, and yet I don't. There's the tower where the sniper killed those people, but I may have read about that." He looked around the campus. Summer school was over, and the fall semester had not yet begun, so it was almost deserted. "I just don't know."

"Well," she sighed, "let's get a hotel room, and we can start fresh tomorrow."

"That's a good idea. I think we should begin with the museums. Surely someone is missing a curator or will recognize a lost historian."

She maneuvered her way through the busy streets and pulled into the covered drive of a high-rise hotel. A uniformed doorman came around to open her door and to see to their luggage. The double glass doors slid open as they approached, and they went into the luxurious lobby. A thick blue carpet over a cream marble floor padded their steps to the desk.

The manager smiled when he recognized Maya. "Your usual room, Ms. Kingsley?"

"Yes, please." She signed the register, and he gave her an unmarked card key to unlock her door.

The bellman and their luggage led the way to the glass elevators half-hidden by lush greenery. "You come here often?" Adam teased.

"Yes, I do, and always on business," she retorted.

The elevator swooped them up to the penthouse, and the bellman silently moved the bags into the spacious closet. Adam went to the window and gazed out at the view. "Not bad," he said with a grin. "Where's the bed?"

She opened the double doors to show him the rest of the suite. "Will you stop it? The bellman is going to think you're my sweet thing."

"Oh, how times have changed." Adam tipped the bellman and closed the door. "So you think he'll assume I'm a gigolo?"

"You're handsome enough for one."

"Oh? You sound as if you know that for a fact."

"I've seen my share of movies," she said with a laugh.

"No sleigh bed. What a disappointment. Maybe room service could bring one up."

She unbuttoned her beige linen jacket and slipped it off. Her dress was very simple, with a beige skirt and a white jewel-necked top. She wore her hair in an intricate bun on the back of her head. Adam watched her in fascination. "Here's a new Maya to add to my collection. The jet-set *patrona*, accustomed to elegance and champagne and suites that cost a small fortune." He came up behind her and slowly lowered her zipper. "We have a while before dinner."

"I thought you'd be tired after last night. And then there was the drive over here." Her gray eyes seduced him in the full-length mirror on the wall.

He met her gaze over her shoulder and gently pulled the dress away. "I know a perfect way to relax."

Maya stepped out of the dress, and he draped it over the back of a chair, then removed her half-slip before unsnapping her bra.

"God, you're beautiful," he said as he studied her reflection. He reached around her to cup both her breasts. Maya's head rolled back on his shoulder, and she kissed the underside of his jaw.

"Come to bed with me," Adam breathed. "Let me love you."

With a seductive smile, Maya went to turn down the bed and then stepped out of her tan-and-white high-heeled shoes. Adam had undressed quickly, and she smiled again to see that he was already eager for her.

He sat on the edge of the bed and ran his hands over her silken thighs and hips. "The inventor of panty hose should have been shot."

She laughed softly as he stripped the hose and her panties away. Lifting her arms, she pulled the pins from her hair and let it fall down her back and brush against her hips as Adam drew one of her nipples into his mouth. She threaded her fingers through his thick hair as he moved his head to love the other breast. "That feels so good," she murmured.

"If you think this feels good, just wait," he promised huskily.

He drew her down onto the bed and spread her hair out like a corolla behind her head. "My Maya, my beautiful love. My enchantress." Lowering his head, he kissed her lips tenderly, then with growing passion.

Maya stroked the smooth muscles of his body. "You've always reminded me of a puma," she murmured, "or maybe a Thoroughbred. All sleek muscles and very, very masculine grace." She ran her tongue along the firm crest of his shoulder. "You taste so good."

"I love you," he said with a low current of urgency. "I love you."

"I love you, too."

He entered her smoothly and began to draw out her passion as they gazed into each other's eyes. In his peripheral vision he saw their images in the mirror, and the sight stirred him to even greater passion.

Deeper and more intensely they loved, a sense of immediacy driving them harder and harder. Maya saw the passion and love mirrored in Adam's eyes and watched as his eyes grew subtly darker as he immersed himself in pleasing her.

She moved with him, stroking, licking and kissing his body and lips. She felt him holding back, waiting for her, and the feel of his barely leashed passion thrilled her. Holding nothing back, she rushed to her completion, and when she did, she moved against him so that he moaned softly and joined her in a mutual culmination.

"Adam, I love you so," she sighed against his chest as he held her in the afterglow of their intense loving.

"I love you, Maya. I always will."

Neither mentioned the urgency they had experienced. Both knew that each time they made love could be the last time.

Chapter Fourteen

Maya sat cross-legged on the bed, the morning sun streaming over her loose silk caftan of emerald, turquoise and rose, as she copied the names and addresses of every museum in Austin from the telephone book. Since Adam was still in the shower, she turned on the television and selected one of the popular morning talk-shows.

She followed the news segments and interviews with her eyes, but her mind was engrossed with what the day might bring. Surely today or tomorrow would give them information on Adam's past. Deep inside she felt a dread certainty that they were on the right track.

Lying back on the plump pillows, she thought of what that would mean. Adam still asserted that he had the choice of staying with her, but Maya wasn't willing to give him that option. Although it hurt her, she thought of the idyllic family scene he had described. To leave a wife for her was more than Maya's conscience would allow. To leave a wife and children was even worse. Maya bit her lower lip as she told herself she would have to be the strong one. If Adam was indeed married, she would have to be the one to end it. But could she do it?

She stroked the pillow where Adam's head had rested and thought of the way they had made love before dinner, and again in the silence of the night. She loved Adam as if he were the other half of her being. How could she let him go? Wasn't their love more important than anything else?

Then she thought of the children with eyes as green as Adam's, and she knew they were more important. Once his memory returned, Adam might discover he loved that woman with the short blond hair as much as or more than he did Maya.

The shower stopped in the bathroom, and Maya looked through the open door to see Adam drying off with a thick white towel. He was magnificent, she observed. His body was long and lean, like an Olympic swimmer's, and he moved with the grace of someone proficient in the martial arts. He wrapped the towel around his waist and stuck his head into the bedroom. "Your turn."

Maya stood and slipped off the brilliantly colored caftan. She smiled at Adam and saw the nervousness in his eyes that meant he, too, was worrying about what the day might bring. She twisted her hair into a roll on top of her head and adjusted the water. For a few minutes she stood under the stinging spray, letting it relax her muscles and calm her thoughts. Uncle

Garth had warned them not to get their hopes too high over this trip. Chances were excellent that they would return to the Ranata without having learned anything.

Adam blew his hair dry and brushed it into place as he listened to Maya shower. He was almost ready to call the whole thing off and go home to the Ranata. If he ever remembered his past, he could act upon it then. He knew this urge went beyond the syndrome Dr. Kadlecek had described of a patient putting up barriers against letting anyone know about his amnesia due to fright, embarrassment or the vague dread that he might be a criminal. Adam was no longer so sure he wanted a past if it might destroy his present. Instead of trying so hard to remember, he decided to just relax and let it ride.

Maya turned off the water, and he handed her a towel. As she dried her body, Adam shaved, glancing at her provocative form from time to time in the mist-clouded mirror.

In the other room he heard a singing commercial for cat food; then the news program resumed. He was enjoying the domesticity of sharing a bathroom mirror with Maya when the talk-show host mentioned a name that cut into his mind. "Sally," the man said.

Adam leaned on the cabinet beside the sink to steady himself. The show host continued with the interview, but the name was lodged in Adam's brain. *Sally.* Suddenly his knees turned to jelly, and he knew the last name that went with the Sally in his memory. Canton. Sally Canton. Adam knew that name as well as he knew the anguished face staring at him from the mirror. Images of the blond woman sprang to mind.

Sally feeding baby Joey. Sally trying to be brave on little Becky's first day of school. Sally and he teaching Becky to ride her first bicycle, and Joey begging him to read his favorite bedtime story, *Winnie the Pooh.*

He remembered a house of the same type he and Maya had seen in the well-to-do residential area in San Antonio, only this one was here in Austin. He knew how to get there, and he even knew the address—1221 Burdett Street. Adam felt a sinking nausea as the knowledge swept over him.

Maya glanced at his ashen reflection, then stared at him. "Adam?"

In a deadpan tone Adam said, "I remember. Her name is Sally Canton. The children are Becky and Joey, and they live at 1221 Burdett Street."

The towel nearly dropped from Maya's numbed fingers. "Are you sure?"

Their eyes met in the steamy glass. "I'm positive."

He yanked off his towel and tossed it onto the bathroom floor. "I've got to get over there."

Feeling suddenly vulnerable, Maya covered her nakedness with her towel and gripped it so tightly that her knuckles turned white. "Do you know your name?"

"No, but Sally does. I have to find out." He jerked on his clothes and dug through their suitcase almost frantically in search of a pair of socks. "I'm going to take a taxi over there and find out the answers; then I'll come back here." He shoved his feet into his shoes and crossed the room to put his hands on her shoulders.

Maya stared up at him. She had been unable to say a word. Everything had happened so quickly that she couldn't quite believe what she was hearing. His eyes were veiled and cautious as they had been in the beginning, and the muscle in his jaw was knotted.

"I'll be back," he said at last, and then he was gone.

For the space of a heartbeat, Maya stared after him; then she threw the towel down and dressed in the first clothes she found. She scooped up all their belongings, dumped them into the suitcase and left the room. By the time she checked out of the hotel and got directions to Burdett Street, her car had been brought around. Maya was familiar with Austin and had no trouble finding the neighborhood.

The taxi was still at the curb halfway down the block when she rounded the corner and stopped. Adam was standing beside the cab as if trying to make up his mind whether to leave or stay. The driver said something to him, and Adam dug into his pocket for the fare. Maya parked at the end of the street and waited to see what would happen. She told herself she was doing this because Adam could be wrong and he would need a ride back to the hotel, but in her heart she knew he wasn't wrong and that witnessing this reunion would help her to be strong enough to say goodbye.

He walked up the front sidewalk and paused before ringing the bell. When the door opened, a woman with short blond hair stepped out onto the porch. Adam did a double take; then a wide grin spread over his face as he swooped the woman up in a bear hug. Two small children, a girl and a boy, came barreling out of the house and wrapped themselves around Adam's legs.

Maya had seen enough. With tears streaming down her face, she turned the car around and left. As soon as she was out of town, she pressed her foot to the accelerator and whipped down the highway at a speed that was excessive even for her. The road blurred as she cried, but she made no effort to stop the tears or to slow down. Her heart was breaking, and she could think only of reaching the security of her beloved Ranata.

In the west the hazy sky was taking on a bruised hue. Before long, pewter clouds began to pile on the horizon, and she heard the first rumble of thunder. Maya paid it no mind. The man she loved was gone, and nothing else mattered.

She crossed the dry creek bed she had shown to Adam and drove up the steep incline on the other side. The Ranata was only fifteen minutes away at the speed she was traveling.

As she pulled into her drive, the first of the rains hit. Thunder crashed, and buckets of water poured down on the parched land. Maya walked through the downpour as if unaware of it. Lupe met her at the door, her seamed face full of smiles to see the drought broken and the *patrona* safely home.

"Where is Señor Russell?" Lupe asked when Maya closed the door against the rain.

"He stayed in Austin. We were able to find his people." Maya's voice was dull, and she ached all over.

"He will be here for supper, *si*?"

With a great effort she kept her voice level and calm. "No. He won't be coming back." The *patrona* didn't sob on anyone's shoulder, not even Lupe's.

"You will have supper in the dining room? I have *tortilla* soup and *enchiladas*."

"No, thank you, Lupe. I'm not hungry."

Lupe frowned at her mistress and muttered something in Spanish about skinny women who refused to eat good food. She said she would bring some to her anyway. Maya ignored her.

She went onto the patio and walked under the roof's protective overhang as she went to her room. Once inside, she drew the curtains and stood for a minute in semidarkness, the rain pounding on the red tile roof above her head. The room reminded her of Adam. She could hear the echoes of his mellow voice in the rainstorm, and her mind taunted her with the idea that he might step into the room at any moment.

Maya exchanged her wet clothes for one of her Mexican skirts and a peasant blouse. Barefoot, she padded across the thick carpet to open all the curtains. One direction overlooked the rain-spattered pool and courtyard, the other the back patio and the rolling hills beyond. She sat in one of her puffy white chairs and drew her feet up beneath her. The rain obliterated the view of all but the nearest hills, and the trees leaned heavily against the onslaught of rain. Weather in the hill country was often wild and fierce. After the killing drought, this rain would bring severe floods. But she had no concern for her safety or that of her people. The *hacienda* and the *casitas* out back, as well as the barns and outbuildings, were all on high ground. The flooding would be no problem to them, which was fortunate, for she wasn't sure she was in a condition to do anybody any good.

Up the road the dry creek bed became a trickle, then a stream. All at once a torrent of dirty brown water, filled with branches and leaves and clods of grass, roared down the streambed. The water swept over the road and began to inch its way up the flood marker, and still it rained. In no time the formerly dry bed was a raging, impassable river.

Maya picked at her supper, but only because of Lupe's grumbling. A hard knot of misery had settled coldly in her stomach, and she couldn't force food down. Despite the dampness, she sat in the outdoor room and listened to the drone of thunder and the lashing downpour. The air was heavy with wetness like the air in her cave beside the waterfall. She remembered how Adam had braved his claustrophobia to come to her in the cave, even without benefit of a candle. She also remembered the paradiselike days of swimming in the crystal-clear lagoon and making love on the mossy ledge beneath the fern-shrouded cliff. She touched her cheeks and wasn't surprised to find tears there.

The phone rang, and Maya jumped. Lupe answered it and came to Maya, her face happy once again. "*Patrona*, it is Señor Russell."

"Tell him I'm not at home."

"Not at home? But I've already said that you are." A worried frown creased Lupe's face.

"Then tell him I can't be disturbed."

"But, *patrona*—"

"Lupe, I said I won't come to the phone!"

Lupe's lower lip protruded to show her displeasure, but she went back to the phone and gave Adam the message.

Maya stared dismally out at the wet tiles and dimpling pool. Adam Russell was no more. By now he knew his real name and had, no doubt, called to say goodbye. Maya hated goodbyes and avoided farewell scenes even with casual acquaintances. She couldn't bear hearing Adam tell her of his newly reclaimed life. No doubt he wanted to thank her for her hospitality and tell her how much he regretted all that had happened between them. Maya couldn't face that. As for his having divorced this Sally, that seemed impossible in light of the affectionate embrace on the doorstep. No, he was back with his family, where he belonged.

At intervals the phone rang, but after a while Lupe simply repeated Maya's message without disturbing her—the *patrona* was at home but was not to be disturbed.

Maya sat there until night fell. The soft lights of the patio came on at dusk, turning the silver sheets of rain to gold. Lupe offered to stay late, but Maya sent her home. There was nothing she needed that Lupe could get for her. She needed Adam.

Again the phone rang, but she didn't move to answer it. Its jangling persistence set her nerves on edge, as if they were being scoured by sandpaper, but she let it ring. At last it quit, and Maya looked over at it through the glass wall. Perhaps he had given up at last.

The rain continued all night, amid crashing thunder and jarring lightning. Maya couldn't have slept anyway. The bed was too large and cold without Adam in it. She tried to pretend he was in the guest room and no farther away from her than the patio and library. Once in the middle of the night she got up and walked through the dark house to the open door of the guest room. It was empty, as she had known it would be. Fitful flashes of lightning illuminated the colorful bedspread lying neatly over the bed, the flower-filled *kiva* fireplace with its terra-cotta figurines in the niches above. No Adam here.

Maya wandered through the house as if she were one of its ghosts. Never had her home felt so desolate, so empty. Her bedroom felt even more forlorn.

By dawn the storm had slackened, and the thunder rumbled off on its journey toward the Gulf of Mexico. The rain had stopped hammering at the earth, having become more gentle as if it were tired from its frantic activity. In the dull gray light, Maya finally slept.

That day the phone didn't ring at all, and Maya found herself perversely becoming peeved. He hadn't wasted much time in trying to talk to her, she thought painfully. No doubt he was too busy taking up his life where he had left off. She thought of him lying in bed with the blond woman, and she moaned aloud in pain. Lupe looked around the corner to see what was wrong, and Maya pretended to be reading the magazine that was in her lap.

By late afternoon the rain was little more than a delicate patter. Maya sent Lupe home early because she was tired of the older woman's solicitous glances. Again the silence of the house washed over her. Maya had never experienced loneliness to this degree. It was almost like a physical illness. She had never cried so much, not even when Rick and Kathy eloped or when her parents died. Her face felt stiff and swollen.

Because she was alone, she stripped off her clothes and swam naked in the pool as gentle rain made stars on its surface. Back and forth she swam, seeking exhaustion. The cool water soothed her face, and finally her muscles uncoiled. The honeysuckle and jasmine vines that spread upward over the old section of the house looked glossy and clean under the raindrops, and the potted geraniums were washed to new freshness. Maya sat on the stone edge of the pool and wondered if she would ever feel whole again. Rain had come to refresh her Ranata, but the drought had settled in her heart.

After a while she felt uncomfortably cool, so she went inside to dress. She put on a flowing white caftan that billowed silkily about her ankles. The angel sleeves fell back to expose her arms as she brushed her black hair.

Not having anything better to do, she wandered along the patio on the dry walkway to the living room. She paused to touch the telephone, willing it to ring, then pulled her hand away, afraid it might. She turned on the television to break the oppressive silence, then restlessly turned it off again. The coming night and her life seemed to stretch forward endlessly.

When she heard the knock on the front door, Maya leaped to her feet. Her heart pounding, she told herself there was nothing to fear. Possibly it was only Shelley and Ed dropping by for one of their impromptu visits.

Again the pounding came, and this time it sounded imperative. Maya went to the door and automatically put her hand on the emergency button as she opened it.

Adam stood there, his blond hair haloed by the porch light. For what seemed like an eternity, Maya gazed up at him, her love as raw and unveiled in her eyes as the love she saw in his. Then she saw the blond woman behind him, and she tried to slam the door.

Adam caught it before she could shut it, however, and pushed it open as he stepped in. "The Ranata seems to have altered its hospitality rules," he said.

Even in the midst of Maya's distress, the mellow depth of Adam's voice strummed chords within her. Still, she stepped back and lifted her chin defiantly. "I don't need you to teach me manners, although I'm amazed you'd both come here." Her eyes were steely gray as she glanced regally from Adam to the woman.

"I would have been here much sooner, but the road is flooded, and the damned bridge is washed out above La Avenida."

"We had to backtrack all the way to Austin and come by way of Kerrville," the woman said hesitantly.

"I want you to meet somebody, Maya," Adam said, watching her closely.

Maya felt sick inside and as angry as she ever had been in her life. The woman was pretty in a fresh-scrubbed way. Her hazel-green eyes were worried, as if she were half afraid of Maya, and she was more slender and delicate than Adam had described her. Maya felt as if she towered over her. *"Bienvenida, señora,"* she said with frigid politeness. "My home is your home."

Adam looked amused as he said to the woman, "This is Maya Kingsley, *patrona* of the Ranata. Maya, this is Sally Canton. My sister."

Shocked and almost unbelieving, Maya faltered as she repeated, "Sister!"

Sally hurriedly said, "I wanted to thank you in person for taking care of Philip. He's told me all about how he had amnesia and you saved his life. He wasn't due home from vacation for another week, so I had no idea anything was wrong."

"Philip?" Maya asked, looking at Adam in astonishment.

"Philip Ashburn," he explained. "The *A* on my belt buckle stood for my last name, not my first."

"Come in, come in," Maya said, finally stepping aside. "I'll get some coffee. Sit down." She looked again at Sally, then at the man she had known as Adam. "I'll be right back."

She all but ran about the kitchen, making coffee, then decided *sangría* was faster. She grabbed the carafe Lupe had put back from supper, and three glasses. His sister! Maya had never once thought the woman could be anyone other than his wife!

Philip came to meet her as she emerged with the tray. As he took it their hands touched, and she almost dropped it as the electricity leaped between them.

Maya sank down onto the white leather couch opposite Sally, and Philip sat beside her. "Were... There were children?"

"Yes. Becky and Joey. I had to find a sitter for them before we could come," Sally said.

"And then the rains held us up. The creek is a river now. And that reminds me," he added in an angry tone, "why in the hell wouldn't you talk to me on the phone?"

"I hate goodbyes," Maya said lamely.

"I wasn't trying to say goodbye! I was trying to be sure you were all right. Either Lupe doesn't speak English, or she won't speak it to me. All I could get was something about the *patrona* being unable to talk. I was afraid you were hurt.''

''I'm fine,'' she said in a small voice. To Sally she said, ''What's this about a vacation?''

''Philip had gone on a trip to visit the Frontier Times Museum in Bandera; then he was going to San Marcos to do some in-depth studies on the German pioneers there and in New Braunfels. As I said before, I had no reason to think he was missing because he wasn't supposed to come back until school starts.''

''School?''

''I'm a history professor at the University of Texas,'' he explained. ''It's not as glamorous as being a prince or a grave robber, but it explains the odd things I remembered.''

''A college professor! I never would have guessed!'' she exclaimed.

''Thanks,'' he said wryly.

Maya pulled back a bit. ''Why were you vacationing alone?'' She didn't dare ask if he were married. Just because he wasn't married to Sally didn't mean he was single.

''I'm divorced,'' he said quietly. ''It happened last year. No wife, no kids.''

''When my husband was killed last spring,'' Sally said, ''Philip moved in temporarily to help me over the rough spots. My Jim was a police officer, and his death was...unexpected. The kids love their Uncle Phil so much that he stayed throughout the summer. He was still bitter over his divorce and was saying he never wanted another commitment. I was really surprised to hear about you.''

Maya gazed at Philip, her love shining in her eyes. "So you have no ties."

"Only one." He stood and took her hand to pull her to her feet. "Excuse us, Sally. We have something very important to discuss."

He led Maya to the outside room and shut the door behind them. "Are you disappointed? That I'm only a garden-variety professor, I mean. Nothing nearly as adventurous as some of your guesses."

"I'm not disappointed; I'm relieved. What was this tie you mentioned? Is there a fiancée in the closet?"

"Not yet. But if you'll stand still and quit pacing, I might have one."

"What?"

"Marry me, Maya. I know you're way out of my league, but I love you, and I know you love me. What do you think? Could the *patrona* of the Ranata be happy with a mere schoolteacher?"

"There's nothing 'mere' about you," she replied softly. "Yes, Adam, I'll marry you. I mean, Philip. Adam, you don't look at all like a Philip."

He laughed as he put his arms around her. "I can't imagine your calling me anything but Adam." He kissed her lightly, then with more desire. "Do you really want to marry me? Maybe you should take some time to think it over."

"I've thought about nothing but you for weeks. I don't need time."

"I guess we'll have to live in Austin during the week for this first semester. That will give the university time to replace me."

"Replace you?"

"I'd rather be here on the Ranata. You wouldn't be happy for long in a city."

"But what about you? Your work?"

"This will give me a chance to write—a second book, that is. Remember the day we spent in the library? There was a very good reason that history book seemed so familiar to me. I wrote it. And I want to write other history books that will make the past come alive for students. I want to write them right here, with you by my side."

"Adam, I love you."

"I love you, my Maya." He bent his head and kissed her as the life-giving rain glittered in the porch light.

* * * * *

Silhouette Romance™

Legendary Lovers Trilogy

BY DEBBIE MACOMBER....

ONCE UPON A TIME, in a land not so far away, there lived a girl, Debbie Macomber, who grew up dreaming of castles, white knights and princes on fiery steeds. Her family was an ordinary one with a mother and father and one wicked brother, who sold copies of her diary to all the boys in her junior high class.

One day, when Debbie was only nineteen, a handsome electrician drove by in a shiny black convertible. Now Debbie knew a prince when she saw one, and before long they lived in a two-bedroom cottage surrounded by a white picket fence.

As often happens when a damsel fair meets her prince charming, children followed, and soon the two-bedroom cottage became a four-bedroom castle. The kingdom flourished and prospered, and between soccer games and car pools, ballet classes and clarinet lessons, Debbie thought about love and enchantment and the magic of romance.

One day Debbie said, "What this country needs is a good fairy tale." She remembered how well her diary had sold and she dreamed again of castles, white knights and princes on fiery steeds. And so the stories of Cinderella, Beauty and the Beast, and Snow White were reborn....

Look for Debbie Macomber's *Legendary Lovers* trilogy from Silhouette Romance: *Cindy and the Prince* (January, 1988); *Some Kind of Wonderful* (March, 1988); *Almost Paradise* (May, 1988). Don't miss them!

SRT-1

ATTRACTIVE, SPACE SAVING BOOK RACK

Display your most prized novels on this handsome and sturdy book rack. The hand-rubbed walnut finish will blend into your library decor with quiet elegance, providing a practical organizer for your favorite hard-or soft-covered books.

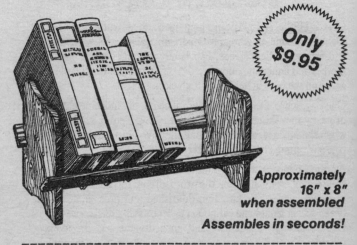

Only $9.95

Approximately 16" x 8" when assembled

Assembles in seconds!

To order, rush your name, address and zip code, along with a check or money order for $10.70* ($9.95 plus 75¢ postage and handling) payable to *Silhouette Books*.

Silhouette Books
Book Rack Offer
901 Fuhrmann Blvd.
P.O. Box 1396
Buffalo, NY 14269-1396

Offer not available in Canada.

*New York and Iowa residents add appropriate sales tax.

BKR-2A

Silhouette Special Edition

COMING NEXT MONTH

#445 THROUGH ALL ETERNITY—Sondra Stanford
Upon colliding with luscious Lila Addison, big Jeffrey Chappel found the
former model kind to strangers but cautious about commitment. He vowed to
win her precious trust, but could he truly offer her his own heart?

#446 NEVER LET GO—Sherryl Woods
Though Dr. Justin Whitmore acted hard as nails, hospital psychologist Mallory
Blake had glimpsed his softer side. As professional awe turned to personal
ardor, Mallory longed to crack Justin's icy facade—and rush right into his
heart.

#447 SILENT PARTNER—Celeste Hamilton
Fiercely independent Melissa Chambers needed bucks, not brainstorms, to
launch her new restaurant. But headstrong Hunt Kirkland, her far-from silent
partner, was full of ideas...for passionate teamwork!

#448 THE POWER WITHIN—Dawn Flindt
Strongman Joe Rustin had saved Tina's life. He then became her exercise coach
and devoted companion—but *not* the lover she longed for. How could she
convince Joe to unleash his powerful inner passions?

#449 RAPTURE DEEP—Anne Lacey
When lovely, treacherous Stacey reentered Chris Lorio's life, buried rage
surfaced...as did memories of rapture in each other's arms. For the long-ago
lovers, the past held bitterness, secrets and, somewhere, sweet promise.

#450 DISARRAY—Linda Shaw
In small-town Finley, Arkansas, little went unnoticed—especially not "good
girl" Barbara Regent's canceled wedding, compromised reputation and
budding romance with a mysterious, untrusted outsider.

AVAILABLE THIS MONTH:

Silhouette Intimate Moments

THIS MONTH
CHECK IN TO
DODD MEMORIAL HOSPITAL!

Not feeling sick, you say? That's all right, because Dodd Memorial isn't your average hospital. At Dodd Memorial you don't need to be a patient—or even a doctor yourself!—to examine the private lives of the doctors and nurses who spend as much time healing broken hearts as they do healing broken bones.

In UNDER SUSPICION (Intimate Moments #229) intern Allison Schuyler and Chief Resident Cruz Gallego strike sparks from the moment they meet, but they end up with a lot more than love on their minds when someone starts stealing drugs—and Allison becomes the main suspect.

In May look for AFTER MIDNIGHT (Intimate Moments #237) and finish the trilogy in July with HEARTBEATS (Intimate Moments #245).

Author Lucy Hamilton is a former medical librarian whose husband is a doctor. Let her check you in to Dodd Memorial—you won't want to check out!

IM229-1R